# KINGDOM OF THE CLOCK

THE HUGH MACLENNAN POETRY SERIES

Editors: Allan Hepburn and Carolyn Smart

Recent titles in the series

*Earth Words: Conversing with Three Sages* John Reibetanz
*Vlarf* Jason Camlot
*Unbecoming* Neil Surkan
*Bitter in the Belly* John Emil Vincent
*unfinishing* Brian Henderson
*Nuclear Family* Jean Van Loon
*Full Moon of Afraid and Craving* Melanie Power
*Rags of Night in Our Mouths* Margo Wheaton
*watching for life* David Zieroth
*Orchid Heart Elegies* Zoë Landale
*The House You Were Born In* Tanya Standish McIntyre
*The Decline and Fall of the Chatty Empire* John Emil Vincent
*New Songs for Orpheus* John Reibetanz
*the swailing* Patrick James Errington
*movingparts* Edward Carson
*Murmuration: Marianne's Book* John Baglow
*Take the Compass* Maureen Hynes
*act normal* nancy viva davis halifax
*aboutness* Eimear Laffan
*twofold* Edward Carson
*Whiny Baby* Julie Paul
*Metromorphoses* John Reibetanz
*Bridestones* Miranda Pearson
*Dreamcraft* Peter Dale Scott
*Water Quality* Cynthia Woodman Kerkham
*Without Beginning or End* Jacqueline Bourque
*White Lily* John Emil Vincent
*Kingdom of the Clock: A Novel in Verse* Daniel Cowper

# *Kingdom of the Clock*

A Novel in Verse

DANIEL COWPER

McGill-Queen's University Press
Montreal & Kingston • London • Chicago

ISBN 978-0-2280-2371-5 (paper)
ISBN 978-0-2280-2481-1 (ePDF)
ISBN 978-0-2280-2482-8 (ePUB)

Legal deposit second quarter 2025
Bibliothèque et Archives nationales du Québec

Printed in Canada on acid-free paper that is 100% ancient-forest-free, containing 100% sustainable, recycled fibre, and processed chlorine-free.

Funded by the Government of Canada | Financé par le gouvernement du Canada | Canada | Canada Council for the Arts | Conseil des arts du Canada

We acknowledge the support of the Canada Council for the Arts.

Nous remercions le Conseil des arts du Canada de son soutien.

McGill-Queen's University Press in Montreal is on land which long served as a site of meeting and exchange amongst Indigenous Peoples, including the Haudenosaunee and Anishinabeg nations. In Kingston it is situated on the territory of the Haudenosaunee and Anishinaabek. We acknowledge and thank the diverse Indigenous Peoples whose footsteps have marked these territories on which peoples of the world now gather.

---

**Library and Archives Canada Cataloguing in Publication**

Title: Kingdom of the clock: a novel in verse / by Daniel Cowper.

Names: Cowper, Daniel, 1981- author

Series: Hugh MacLennan poetry series.

Description: Series statement: The Hugh MacLennan poetry series

Identifiers: Canadiana (print) 20240509374 | Canadiana (ebook) 20240509390 | ISBN 9780228023715 (paper) | ISBN 9780228024811 (PDF) | ISBN 9780228024828 (ePUB)

Subjects: LCGFT: Poetry.

Classification: LCC PS8605.093 K56 2025 | DDC C811/.6—dc23

---

This book was designed and typeset by Marquis Interscript in 9.5/13 Sabon.

McGill-Queen's University Press
Suite 1720, 1010 Sherbrooke St West, Montreal, QC, H3A 2R7

Authorized safety representative in the EU: Mare Nostrum Group BV, Mauritskade 21D, 1091 GC Amsterdam, the Netherlands, gpsr@mare-nostrum.co.uk

for my grandmother
Joan Diane Anastasiou

THE TWENTY-FOUR HOURS

KINGDOM OF THE CLOCK

## FIRST LIGHT

Who wakes in the kingdom? Gulls tick
on dark winds, the moon's disc dims.

Switches click. Wheels spin. In stacks
of glass and steel five million citizens

still sleep. Dawn nears. Clocks will mete out time
in twenty-fourths, measure moments

by the pace at which hearts beat
and break. The dictates of the clocks

will wake the citizens and send them off
down rain-slick walks to work or school,

while wants that warm each breath
will send quick feet in a race to slake

their daily needs and whims. To chase
the chalice of art or other addiction

down blocks of asphalt street. To veil
the fear of death with wealth or defy

that fear with humdrum chores of love.
Whatever routes they take, like skaters carving

new ice with sharpened blades they'll make
desire lines we can trace.
Vanessa slips

from Connor's bed. It's his loft
so she bathes first and dresses while he sleeps,

swabs cheeks with rouge, sweeps blackened wax
through lashes. Pink, tidy hands repack

her overnight bag with each cosmetic
as it's used. A newcomer from the prairie,

Vanessa still cringes when each daybreak
reveals the chisel-blades of mountain

chipping the sky to a closet's ceiling.
She turns from the walled-in view to scan

Connor's sleeping face (slack,
Siddharthic on the pillowcase)
*What am I*

*to him?* Vanessa thinks, *He's richer every day,*
*profiled for magazines as magnate-in-making –*

*I'm a failed actress, fine barista, washed*
*at twenty-nine –*
pulls on her lilac Vans, spooks

a flock of red-faced finches as she exits
by the balcony. Down a shaky ladder

she clambers to street level, to curbs
where raccoons (half-bear, half-lemur) sprint

for the safety of their dens while she
flits off for Arque Café to don her apron, restock,

open up before the first commuters knock.
Under the rims of fringed slopes and peaks

what's there to see? Minuscule raindrops
flicker past sodium streetlights. Convoys

of crows fly, cawing and cawing over
the mess of right-angled walls and windows,

slant porch-roofs, fire-escapes linking suite
to suite like scaffolds, converted attics

like Connor's accessed illegally by ladders.
If you hold your ear to the hollow polisphere

what's there to hear? Water clicking from trees
to streets, pairs of bloodless feet

padding parquet and tile; electric kettles fizzing
on counters; percolators spitting drips

into stained carafes. Toilets gulp, showers spray,
toasters *ding* when their springs release,

bowls flecked with cereal clink in sinks
and seagulls keen.

Connor squints

as the ladder's rattle wakes him. Knowing
the chatter of returning finches means

Vanessa's left, he rolls from mattress to floor
to fridge door, pulls out a Red Bull – sips

his breakfast by the window. His focus
switches between the dark landscape outside

and his bleary, slowly self-erasing
likeness on the glass. He yawns. He knows he'll need

good energy today to sell a team of visiting VCs
on shares in Omniopticon. Connor

feels twitchy pitching a pump 'n' dump, wishes
he didn't greet each dawn scared the cops

were on to his con, but – can't stop now: with O-Con
a hit, and he and Jack standing to split

obscene riches when they jump ship. Connor
selects Eminem's beat, throb, and pop

from his fire-up playlist. He chants along
to immerse himself in its stress and emphasis

while he showers, soaps his jaw and shaves, dresses,
knots his iridescent tie, pats Rogaine

on his thinning patch. As "Lose Yourself" loops,
repeats its rhymes, Connor fidgets at

the Kleenex scrap clotted to his shaving cut
and with his other hand, pockets the Tiffany ring box

he's kept secret for weeks, waiting for
the right moment to coalesce.
Who owns

a view? The binner who drinks at dawn pays
nothing to watch herons with necks cocked

like flintlocks, the silhouettes of long-necked
gantry cranes along the docks. He watches

the queue of ships load and unload
and feels enthroned on the parapeted

parkade where he sits, with gulls squabbling
in the empty stalls, and police, in response

to empties exploded on the sidewalk below
in starbursts of glass shards, already stomping

up the stair.
On the top floor of an office block,
an old stock-exchange shark takes breakfast

at his desk, absorbing the same McMuffin meal
he's ordered for forty years. Circadian clock

synced to New York, Murray feels his jowls quiver
as he chews. He focuses on his proprioceptions,

hoping they'll disintegrate the shade
of dreams in which he'd eluded death

by having his consciousness coded, uploaded
to some satellite. There, in ephemeral forms

he'd frolicked with other digitized tycoons
and sprites. At first, their orgies were as purely

ecstatic as the Kama Sutra-esque sculptures of
tantric temples, each orgasm repeatable at will –

but the virtual Eden regressed to circuitry,
and soon his code was chased 'round wafers

of silicon by suckers who'd been zeroed out
on trades he rigged, morphing into cattle dogs

that clawed his naked skin. Murray lifts his gaze
to watch the night slide west across the sea.

Nips of rye slowly rinse the taste of sickness
from his gullet, stretched out by years

of swallowing things whole. Murray
knows living on the world's periphery

lets a few like him amass vast fortunes
but consigns most citizens to waking late,

completing unnoticed work while the world's masters
dine and go to bed. *Where would we be*

*without the sea,* he thinks. *Peaks and deserts,*
*a patchwork of woods and bogs estrange our hours*

*from other hours, enforce the rule:*
*chronology is destiny*. Descendants'

sheepskin degrees adorn the walls like trophies.
A colourized portrait of his mother

aged six and dressed as Bo Peep, a shot
of his father's butcher shop and LCD

where digital pics of grandkids cycle,
reproachful mothers and grandmothers

cropped carefully out. *What's it all for?*
Murray wonders. His hordes of holdcos

will be disbanded when he dies, their spoils
plundered by a dozen offspring. He's vexed

to think how his brothers and brothers' sons
still share the butcher shop, stuff sausage links

out front with a hand-cranked machine, chop
lambs up on a table by the till, ask

after each customer's affairs as if they cared.
Halos
glowing over closed ski runs waste their ghost-light

on urban barriers, on baffled waves, on
the navigation deck of a gearless

Panamax being guided into Port. Grey light
glitters on the pilot's white stubble,

as Enoch, working the graveyard shift,
docks one last ship for the night in its slip,

arthritic hands clasped behind his bony back.
Friends from the Port Police buzz him home,

his rickety frame leaping neatly from their launch
to his live-aboard sailboat, a derelict

sloop moored to a lonely buoy. Bloodstream
stinging in his thawing hands, Enoch unpeels

the wax shell from a puck of Babybel,
eats it with some crackers and goes to bed.

Likenesses he painted of his ex and their son
are pinned above his bunk: Anna

in a ponytail, young enough to be
his estranged daughter; Samson separated from him

by five decades like a grandson. Enoch dozes.
Stevedores lift cargo from the vessel he docked.

Winches clink, reel chains in link by link.
Containers are loaded on railcars,

clank east on train tracks to dollar stores
and sprawling malls. Daylight grows behind

mountains to the east. Polka bands
of crows tune up in parks

and swampers flick on four-ways,
dolly pastry crates into cafés. Enoch

joins the other sleepers in a recurring dream
all citizens share
where rising tides

overtop thresholds, invasive waves bump
buoyant throw pillows on ceilings, float beds

over balcony railings out to sea on the ebb tide
so all night oneironauts dot the ocean swells

sailing for shores they'll never reach.
On cue
millions of bedside cell phones buzz, trill

with cheerful songs to start the day.
Fake chimes rouse the rest. Matte coals ignite

in scads of frontal lobes, irradiate
cryptic sights of fleets and reefs, far beaches,

bleach out those visions like Fujifilm
exposed to sun. The morning skyline

of bleak blues and greys solidifies, studded
with more and more candescent squares as

citizens rise. Gulls whirl off winds into
dripping pews of trees, paper-white gorgets

flashing in the first flicks of sun that breach
mountain peaks to brush the city

with golden brooms, sweep the pointed shadows
of gnomonic pines, towers, and ships' masts

west towards the sea. Far underground,
tectonic clocks *tick tock,* store up their forces

for an overdue quake.
When the Big One hits,
will our stacks of glass and concrete sway

like shaken trees or snap like bamboo sticks?
We'll see. If the kingdom's on borrowed time,

then so are we. So is all of this
except the double-sexed deities

of ocean and orogeny. Tender organs
of vapour and quilled hills rub and rut nightly,

begetting shoals of blind raindrops that seep
down slopes above the kingdom of the clock.

## DAYBREAK

In hills above the kingdom of the clock
rain tops up a reservoir, hisses down the spillway

in endless excess, snakes past nursing homes
and railyards to lick sand into shifting bars

in the tidal rip. Here at the river's lips
and the reservation's shoreline, Ken wades

hip-deep with the other fishers.
Reel after reel whirrs when the wrist's twist

flings line and lure, click-clicks as the line's retrieved.
*Come fishie, come,* Ken chants. *Fishie, come taste*

*what I've thrown you.* Chum kelts gone zombie cruise
the surface, bump against men's rubber waders

with snouts so scuffed their skulls are sticking out.
Ken knows where shining Coho and Pinks

swim in place, sipping the mineral signature
of spawning grounds washed downstream. He knows

they don't yet know they're summoned by that taste
to unleash armaments of cells and genes,

scatter roe and milt into stirred gravel,
trigger their own dissolutions. There's a code

in the slow flutter of their gills, Ken knows,
a chorus that cries:
*We wait. We left our sea*

*to chase a scent. It led us here. We wait.*
Ken feels lips on his lure; his wrist jerks back

to set the hook in a coho's kype. Friends
cheering, Ken wallows backwards to the beach –

keeps the line tight when the fish runs, till
the salmon's rose and silver blade slaps mud,

the discs of its beached eyes stare blindly,
unable to focus in the alien medium of air

and Ken's knifepoint stabs between their orbits,
cracks the brain case open with a snap. Ken flops

the shivering fish onto the bed of ice
in his Coleman cooler, pops the lid closed. Soles

squelching in his leaky waders, he walks back
into the waves, re-casts, reflects upon a tone

in his friends' cheers he didn't hear before
being outed: a correlate to his friend's eyes

hunting for some telltale of his newly known
secret.
        But what's it all for if not

to weave us into a web of knowing
and being known? Ken's sister's kids wake

in beach-side tents, leave by kitchen doors
to angle and applaud for fish whose forebears

their forebears ate. Everyone joins in when
the refreshed river invites salmon to surge

upstream and risk the ancient gauntlet
of walls and weirs, pens and panniers and nets.

Blood-slopped gloves of fish-cleaners will toss guts
in high arcs for eagles to snatch at apogee

while children gasp; sisters and mothers
jar chunks with berry drupelets in oil,

smoke pink filets and sugar-dry nuggets.
A suspension bridge spans the sky above

band land, displaying a rival signal
in reflected high beams flashing up its cables

as commuters pass.
Outside an office trailer
band council rents out, a grey mob of rock doves

alchemize to flashing tin, flapping from puddles
to roosts under the bridge deck, alarmed by

the black Ford Ranger pulling in. Headlights
flash across ADANAC PLUMBING stencilled

on the trailer's side, where, by dry-stacked stairs
of cinderblocks, the driver stops to drop his wife.

Coral tugs Mark's thorny beard to wish him luck,
swings off the bench-seat with a swish

of coffee-coloured hair. Their black pickup
turns back onto the street, fan belt squeaking

as it does on damp mornings. She enters,
re-locks the vinyl door, rotates dusty

blinds to admit the silver light. She didn't like
the glance Mark's eyes gave themselves

in the side mirror. When her father's gaze
glinted like that, it meant he'd not be home

from playing craps till morning's light,
the adrenaline of total loss

lofting from him like steam. Anxiously
she texts *I love you! Be good today!* to Mark.

He sends back, when he stops at the first red light,
a string of reassuring hearts. She's set

a timetable for the day: sites to hit,
new jobs for Mark to quote while Coral keeps

the books, takes calls, dispatches trucks.
As she processes mail, inputs bills

and cheques, she finds a slim package for herself,
a plastic mother of pearl phone case,

over-printed with peachy roses. She snaps it
around her phone – admires its elegance

as passing dump trucks shake her office walls.
She watches waxwings pick berries clockwise

around the dirt lot's plastic-slat periphery, but
workdays never go like clockwork for Coral:

Jaswahl's wife phones in to say last night
Jas wrapped his Silverado round a pole.

*Is he okay?* asks Coral.
*Fine, just fine,*
Parm answers stiffly, so Coral says *Take care,*

and thanks her for calling. Coral notes
in her calendar to send a casserole,

dials Mark to discuss if they'll reassign or rebook
Jas's jobs. It goes to voicemail. She texts.

No response. *Lord in Heaven,* she sighs, pulls up
Find My iPhone on Mark's Mac,

sees the icon blip atop the casino. She swears,
starts dialling up their other guys

to squeeze Jas's jobs into their days.
Some squawk, some seem almost glad. She allocates

the extra sites to Mark and texts her husband
*I know where you are!* adds angry emojis

that somehow soften her mood, trigger
a twinge of pity. On screen, the pulsing

circle begins to shift as Mark jogs
to where he left his Ranger parked, and Coral

calls that suddenly kinetic circle
*liar* and *dogfucker*, she calls it *loser*

without a lick of guilt.
From public gardens
where they sleep, panhandlers commute

to concourses and curbs to seine haul
the common crowd. Glen bins, he doesn't beg,

so he can hang around the encampment,
watch city workers with reacher grabbers

collect sharps and wrappers, soiled surgical
face masks. Glen wipes sleep from his lashes,

adjusts his Rodman-era Bulls jersey,
taps the tarp lean-to he waits beside.

Droplets lisp down the plastic weave
and Glen whispers: *Brooklyn?*

*Are you coming out today? Last night I dreamed*
*the sky was full of horns, and the sea*

*drained away, sank out of sight. You and me*
*walked down the empty ocean floor*

*and found old longhouses lumpy with anemones,*
*crumpling without the water pressure there*

*to hold them up but full of gold.*
*A snake lived there with a gangrene penis,*

*and it made babies born with gangrene.*
*Did you sleep well? Did you dream*

*prophetic dreams?*
No word in answer. Glen
looks up at the flimsy clouds, and thinks

*Nice roofing weather*, remembers mornings
on job sites with his dad and brother Ken,

how wisps rose from thermoses like chimneys,
how mists breathed from men's mouths

after each slurp of sweetened coffee. He recalls
dinners on his sister Donna's deck, steam

rising from the seams of tinfoil crimped
round salmon filets, cold beers doled out

by mom and dad until the stars fell like a fog.
When tired, he toddled to the backyard shed

Donna's husband remodelled as four walls
for Glen to live in, to plaster with the posters

he adored of late-stage Dennis Rodman
pierced, inked, and dyed like an Aztec priest.

It makes him ache, thinking of those times
before one night's drunken euphoria

had led him into the bedroom of Donna's eldest girl
and –
        *What'd I do, to make her run and scream?*

*Sit on her bed and ask about her dreams?*
He relives the fallout: a scene with Donna

and David like burning bonfires, his pained
mother, father smoothing rough waters

by asking Glen to live with Ken instead,
who had no kids, no daughters for him to scare.

He'd shocked them all by sneering
                                        *I won't share*

*a roof with a queer*
                        and mocked them

with *What, you didn't know?*
                                    Bloody-nosed
he'd fled his brother's brick-like fists

across the reserve, slowing only to croak
through windows left ajar:
                                *Ken's gay! Big fag!*

until he reached the bridge, and clomped alone
across the pearly sky and back to streets

where he'd slept before.
                            *But why should I*
*have kept Ken's secret? So Mom and Dad could go on*

*loving him more than me?*
                                Under the curse
of more love than he deserves, Glen cracks

the lid off his wake-up bottle of rice wine,
tilts out a sunrise swallow.
At the sandbar,

Ken's reeling in another Pink. Their father
had three kids, and it's the son who got away

he asks for most as he fails in palliative care –
not smiling Donna or dutiful Ken who sit

and make him grin as long as they can
to give their mother a break, let her nap

on the hospital couch nearby. The old woman
never leaves his room now, afraid to let him

slink away unprayed-for as sick cats and old men
like to do –
so he drips through her fingers

like the dozens of grated streams
which sink suspended salts into the sea's

submerged and scattered mouths, dispensing
the telltale taste of the kingdom's chemistry.

## COMMUTE

Ignoring the telltale taste of municipal chemistry
Anna sips her tea, scoops out avocado flesh

to share with her son, sprinkles the green lumps
with sugar and citrus while their puppy Pom

Percival snaps at her pantleg. Anna
tucks the Italian wool away from his needle teeth,

thinking how beautiful her son Samson is
as she watches him chew – resembling

her father listening to the morning news
when he's at peace like this.
                                        Her hair's worn

in a barrister's lob these days, not a ponytail,
and she preens for court as her grandmother

preened for church. Dog fur on pant cuffs
doesn't impair her coiffure, couture –

her jacket's fit, her flax-flower silk blouse
puffed blue between butter-yellow lapels

will be what rivals and colleagues see. But even
as she eats with Samson, Anna's inner

chamber where she rehearses legal arguments
or tactics to deal with possible attacks expands,

occludes other thoughts –
                                        she rises to leave,
needing another hour at her desk to prep.

Samson, she says, must get himself to school
on time, be good, his dad will pick him up.

*No getting into trouble!* No telling when
her work will end. And when Percival's jaws

clip at her cuff again, she hops,
stiletto heel crunching a fluffy paw. The Pom

screams. Samson screams. Shushing them
with *Sorry, Sorry!* and saying *I'll miss my bus!*

she slams the door and sprints to the bus stop,
shoes skidding on algal sidewalk. Her ride

arrives, wrapped with wristwatch ads of film stars
in dressage kit. Anna's panting as she boards,

taps her pass on a recalcitrant,
mute sensor. The driver nods, coughs, steers through

skid row where plywood windows pair off against
glittering sheets of condo curtain wall

that show, like screensavers, gliding icons
of innumerable gulls. Payday loan-shops,

gang-run diners and dispensaries give way
to rainbow crosswalks where men in zebra faux fur

plod to local coffee shops before the bus
attains the precincts of doormen, museums,

kitsch cafés where sparrows hop between
patrons' cordovan shoes. Scanning the bus

like the closed-circuit cameras cupped
in plastic globes, Anna spots pubescent girls

in uniforms swaying among the commuters
as she once did, thigh-level pleats attracting looks

no matter how unformed the limbs within.
She's reminded of Enoch's slim sailboat

tossing on choppy seas, of tottering
between stacks of books always poised

to topple, pots of paint always seeking
to spill – she, used to his weakening frame,

and Enoch familiar with her youth. Watching
men eye tweens, Anna wonders *What's it all for*

*if gazers don't glance away, remember*
*how they ought to behave?* She stares outside,

tries reading billboards that invite marks
to monetize, anonymize. Her mind

wanders, brainstorming slogans for the city:
"Pity is justice, justice pity." "White

blossoms look like skulls. Let's green the city."
Her bus hisses, halts at the train station. Anna

marches with discharged crowd to a platform
where those waiting keep apart like twigs

in shy canopies of trees, swipe candled screens
from meme to meme while between the rails

squeaking mice lick the greasy or sweet insides
of wrappers. *What's it all for, if not*

*to let us go safely among strangers?*
wonders Anna, in the crush another busload brings.

*All the same, Enoch was right to say*
*it'd be cruel to make us live this way*

*if we weren't free, if we didn't have*
*virtual worlds to fill with effigies*

*of what we'd like to be.*
Anna tries
to concentrate on court, plan out

canned answers for the judge's questions, but feels
down, fears a bone in Percy's paw is snapped

and he'll whimper alone while she helps
rich crooks play tug-of-war over windfall gains

and Samson strings out after-school hours
with his cryptic father. *What's it all for?*

Anna asks again, as life hacks, listicles
of cutest pets, commands to cucks

to cultivate their horns proliferate online
like algae in vernal sunshine.
*I repent*

*my imperfections,* one ape types into his profile,
*unsightly hairs, my pores and oils. Forgive me*

*this girdle of fat, these scars, these lumps*
*of rehealed bones. Grant me your likes. Swipe right.*

Half-distracted by thoughts of work, by memes
and chattering earbuds, each self-aware

chimera in the station assesses the others
as prospective mates and rivals, compares

clarities of skin and sclera, auras
and pheromones. Then whether there's cause

or only correlation, many minds
synchronize unknowingly, unite

in wondering: *How'd we get this way,*
*souls dug into us like ants in sandy clay?*

*Could we be stripped of selfhood by natural process*
*or black miracle, transformed to ghostless*

*machines? O Lord,* each petitions, self-pity
moving them to prayer, *however these souls first formed,*

*let them thrive, let their anchors and branches ramify,*
*thread deeper in* – until, one by one,

each rebels against these alien ideas,
startled into asking
*wait – am I thinking*

*my own thoughts still or has some malware*
*seized control?*
Stooping in confusion back

to apps and podcasts, commuters snuff
flickering candlewicks which linked them to strange spirits,

scared to be burdened with bad data
too contraband to keep, too secret to delete –

except Anna, who lets the moment complete,
allows her eyes to focus past the fenceposts

and wire mesh that keep wild animals
from walking on the tracks, skim past

the daisy-studded grass and grey skyline
beyond to indescribable indicia

of forms circling on solar winds, collecting
and dispensing grace. When Anna sits at her desk,

she'll scribble what she witnessed
before the day's monotony can whitewash

what she felt, rewrite the messages she received.
She'll never speak aloud about ecstatic sights

or theosophies implied in gaps
between knives and fins, in declivities

between cups and wings. She drank them in, and now
will keep the card she wrote on secret,

hidden safely in her purse until perplexed
executors unfold it when she dies.

## OFFICES

*When will I die?*
Feng sits on her entry bench
listening to the grown daughter who lives downstairs,

poised to rise when she hears Meghan emerge
so Feng can greet her only child at least

once between dawn and dawn. Iterative sounds
from the basement suite betray Meghan's movements –

the springs of the hide-a-bed where Meghan sleeps
creak each time she sits, each time she stands.

Feng's amazed how many times her daughter
absent-mindedly slides the same drawer

open and shut, open and shut, shut, shut.
*Click, click* go Feng's fingernails as she flexes

each painted oval against her thicker thumbnail,
as if checking off a list. Sounds downstairs

cohere into an overcoat's rustle, grunts
as her daughter pulls on boots, a squeak

as the basement door is eased agape.
Feng darts outside as she hears her daughter halt –

hesitate – before stumping angrily up her steps
in Michelin-man puffy coat, hands pushed ahead

in pockets as if she were pointing pistols.
*How'd you sleep, bao bei?* asks Feng, but Meghan

only shakes her parka's hood. They file down the front path
without speaking, clump down a few steps

to street level. *Can I give you a ride?* Feng offers,
fishing out her fob. *Where are you off to?*

Her Acura beeps and flashes its lights, the locks pop.
*Leave me alone,* Meghan moans, hustling away downhill.

When Feng drives by a minute later,
she sees her daughter slowed to a shuffle, shouting

into her phone. Dismayed at how she scarcely
saw Meghan's face in their encounter, ashamed

at her inability to help her daughter,
tears puff up Feng's eyelids, her nose

begins to run. Breathing deep to sop up
unwelcome thoughts, she blinks at dashboard dials

and presses play. An oratorio flows
from the Acura's speakers. Feng's panic relaxes

as familiar notes group themselves in phrases,
rehearsing a colloquy whose thematics

she can grasp.
                        Crews of crows thread overhead.
Straggling drivers stop and start on highways

overhung by pine trees where passerines sing,
as workers in Hi-V vests spin lollipop signs

to start and re-stop lanes. Drumming thumbs
on steering wheels in time to FM beats,

drivers rock in stationary seats, each
torn between putting the car in park

and leaning on the horn. Stop and go. Stop
and go, while radios repeat the blare

of weather updates, news, Led Zeppelin riffs,
a satellite shock-jock's banter with porn stars,

a local zoo-crew's sound effects, the traffic
chopper's whine.
Safely parked downtown,

Feng waits in line at Arque Café, watches
men take turns reciting morning orders

to Vanessa. Each receives her wide-eyed
smiles of thanks, savours her radiance

before sidling aside, irrelevant
while drinks are made. Feng's pained to see men's hands

crinkle small bills in the tip jar, slip cards
across the till, wishes her own daughter

had Vanessa's looks, had suitors who wouldn't
pop in and out, but want to offer

a home, security, some cared-for kids.
Feng watches men's hopeful eyes watch slim

fingers collect their love-notes, pop paper chits
with come-ons and phone digits

into an apron pouch; she'd be relieved
to know Vanessa's smile's on autopilot;

her inner self's rehearsing dialogue
from the unstageable script she's writing,

or reluctantly picturing futures
she and Connor might share, with Hermès purses,

lacrosse-playing boys and a daughter she'd scold
for purging after meals.
Post rush, Vanessa

will shuffle her cards, read aloud what's penned
on the backs to make co-workers laugh

and text the worst one-liners to Connor, who
shoots back clever, if cruel, codas.
                                        What's it all for

if not to let Feng's high heels clink-clank
steel plates slung over maintenance trenches –

to let Feng wait at the crosswalk
with warm to-go cup cozy in her grip

under a poplar sapling where an owl
is trying not to panic while it waits

for night? When the walk sign
blinks its green figurine, Feng skips between

Dictator Chic sedans running the red light
to enter her building's echoing atrium

where a chrome pendulum swings from wall
to window. To envy is mortal; to lord it,

divine. Feng likes to picture a perfect city
for perfect people, but ideal citizens

are far off or fictional while flawed specimens
fill lobbies, watch elevator numbers

flick down to L. Headlines alternate
on ad-screens on the way up, providing free

schadenfreude to riders with idle eyeballs:
        *Influencer dead in free-birth fiasco.*

        *Bikini hiker lost down Swiss crevasse.*
Otis doors hum open, slide shut with a bump.

That owl Feng spotted in the sapling – lost
in man-made space without hope of return

to the farmland where it belongs –
strikes her as an apt symbol of the dark

prognosis since Meghan's third episode,
that psychosis would recur, each "normal"

stretch shorter, less normal than the one before,
until a break that wouldn't knit, a final rip

no stitch could fix. Feng's thumbnails click
her fingernails like a sequence of switches, until

she forces her fingers apart, compels herself
to formulate a to-do list for the day, wargame

her morning appointments.
Refreshed in his garden
camp, Glen taps the tarp again, calls

*Brooklyn, can you hand me out my pills?* Spider eggs
stick to the garden's chicken-wire,

gossamers glue tulip to tulip like kisses.
Glen's thick lashes blink back tears

from seeing the prosperity in every garden path
where garter snakes lie glazed with surplus skin

and the slugs they hunt rest safely in sunless nooks.
Ants shift grain by grain in daisy chains

of legs and feelers. *Sister Ants,* Glen scolds,
*why slave so hard? There's always dew for Sister Snake*

*to drink, always slugs for her to swallow.*
*But honour the ants' labour, Sister Snakes.*

*Something's sacred in their striving to guard*
*their President, brew fermented sweets*

*for nieces from the teats of rose-mites,*
*expand and excavate their nest –*
*Foolish!*

Glen hears the garter snakes hiss: *Ants*
*imitate living things, but there's no souls*

*in those automata, no life. Crush one*
*and nothing but a whiff of vinegar comes out.*

*We know: our split tongues drink the dew*
*and speak nothing but truth.*
Glen bites his lip,

remembering how Donna and Ken
picked up the slack when their dad got sick,

while Glen felt aimless, saddened
by their incomprehensible efficiency. *Brooklyn,*

he calls, *you ever waking up? Can I*
*at least come in to get my pills?*
No response.

Foregoing his morning dose of Seroquel,
Glen leaves, hoping his shopping carts are still

where he hid them.
Phones begin to ring on lesser desks.
Underlings duck looks from muck-a-mucks,

check vibrating phones on laps, select
emojis to answer with a tap. On computer screens,

we toggle backgrounds tones in spreadsheets,
polish overdue deliverables while

carpeted foyers fill and teams trade decks.
At Omniopticon, Connor's guiding

prospective investors through his pitch deck,
silver and gold necktie snaking down his chest.

Too big for his chair, Connor's boss Jack sits
like a small mountain as Connor clicks

through the slideshow, watching his prey react
to words like "disruptive" "proprietary" "unparalleled"

used to puff products Jack and Connor know
aren't real. Murray sits nearby – not part

but patron of the VC team. A one-man claque,
he gravely nods as Connor talks,

acts gobsmacked when Connor displays
a slick mock-up of surveillance tech

identifying citizens by gait
and skeletal ratios. Inside, Murray's

skeptically amused, but he dutifully shakes
his sagging jowls in awe. He's there to push the deal,

earn double finder's fees from Jack
and the gullible VCs. At the final slide,

Connor takes his seat, deftly unbuttoning his jacket
as he sits. Hands flick through printouts of fictionalized

financials disclosed under an NDA.
Outside the boardroom, scores of keyboards

click busily in compact cubicles.
Jack leaps to his feet, huge frame seeming

to block the sixtieth-floor view of cloudy skies,
confides in low, ecstatic tones

how O-Con's tech is piloting in Xinjiang,
Tibet, how a Hong Kong roll-out is in the works,

then – Jack pauses for effect – PRC wide.
He lets that sink in before talking ROI,

an IPO with a sexy ticker. Murray judges
the hook set, excuses himself with a few handshakes

and lets Jack lead his guests through four floors
of coders at plexiglass desks, monitors

prickling with pinyin and simplified glyphs
which Murray discreetly clicks pictures of

as he dodges towards the elevators.
On the tour, Jack winks at Connor, who knows

the joke – O-Con's "employees" are paying
to fill the floor: $40K a pop

for a work visa and route to residency,
no questions asked. They're paying the rent,

working not for O-Con but employers
overseas. Tour complete, the visitors

are dazzled by the sham, thrilled to shake
Jack's heavy hand, wire millions to O-Con's

bank account in exchange for names entered
in a list headed "Members Registry."

*But what's it all for,* Connor asks himself,
*if not to make us rich?*
Courtrooms hush

while clerks duck behind wooden fretworks
to fetch judges. Anna sits erect

at a counsel table, binder open
to her speaking notes, exhibits under

lettered tabs behind – identical white binders
stacked, ready to hand up and across the podium

to opposing counsel. Still feeling
topsy-turvy from the commute, her mind

still fizzes from what she saw. This courthouse,
its tamed, rules-based rituals seem

strange to her again, as it did when she
and Enoch would row ashore, explore

the kingdom's streets like shipwrecked sailors
to watch citizens enact

strange customs. That era's past, those paths
long sundered. And there's no time now for regret

as Anna rises sharply to her feet,
smoothes her jacket's yellow wool, bows.

As the robed judge takes his seat and nods
his bald, Caribbean head, Anna recognizes

in him another shipwrecked relic –
come from the West Indies for law school

sixty years before, when such as him seemed
a marvel to local citizens.

Now he goes leaning on a walking stick.
But Anna waves away these thoughts – rises, says

her name, which litigant for whom she's come.
The workday's underway in the finite city.

## WORKDAY

Work underway, what defines the city?
Landlords make their rounds, push slips

through mail slots whose metal flaps fall back, clicking
after messages drop through. Viró sits

on her bedroom windowsill, watching
ash from the Pall Mall she's smoking float down

into the overgrown back lane below.
*Like snowflakes,* she thinks –
the same pale blue

her hair is dyed. Fumes stroke the old tarred
power pole nearby that's been sawn off, bolted

to a new base to delay replacement, wired
to the building's side so it doesn't tip.

Behind her, an eviction slip lies unopened
on the floor. Sketches on loose sheets, a litter

of wax maquettes bear witness to what obsessed her,
made her ignore her landlord's threats with her bank

account blank.
Last night Viró hung
her system of winged and wingless figurines,

let them fly on tethers of fishing line
that rise to horizontal rods, criss-cross,

flex against supporting, suppressing lines
till they knot around a ceiling hook left over

from when this was a factory. Weeks ago,
Viró confirmed on Reddit that under the RTA

she gets one last chance to pay: thirty days
to clear up rent arrears. Cigarette nearly gone,

dyed hair in her eyes like wisps of alpine sky,
Viró texts the cell repairmen she supplies,

asks for parts lists, special orders, current
prices. She winces, taps cracked glass

with plaster-wrecked fingertips whose cuticles
and quicks still bleed. Viró tallies

the phone screens, the chips, and cameras
she'll need to make rent… and a flight

to the gallery in Phoenix that's keen?
*A girl can dream,* thinks Viró, *but first – flip*

*enough merchandise to keep the room. Then we'll see*
*about a show.* She knows it's touch and go.

She'll do her best, and if that falls short – do
what she needs to do.
                    Viró sips a final puff

from the pack of Pall Malls' last tube and flicks
the spent filter away: watches it flitter

like a de-winged moth into the alley's maze
of blackberry canes and leaves.
                              Someone knocks;

a key invades her lock, clanks the deadbolt
back. The landlord's son Paul walks in, clipboard

in hand, rolling a huge plastic cart
behind him which dings off the doorframe's rim

as it scrapes in. Paul notes the folded
paper untouched on the floor, sniffs the air.

*No smoking in here!*
*I'm not,* says Viró,
climbing back inside.
*Eviction notice,*
he points out.
*I know.*
*Now's part two.*
*I'm here to seize your stuff, for Dad to sell*

*if you can't pay in five days or fewer.*
*Distraint. It's legal.* He flips a fact sheet

on the countertop. Viró picks it up,
but words wash around the page, her gaze

unable to extract meaning. *I thought*
*the Act…*
*You're on a commercial lease,* says Paul.

*Residential rules don't apply.*
*But I live here!*
*Lease says you can't,* says Paul.
*You put that in!*

*You signed it.*
The plastic bin with one lame wheel
limps around the concrete floor while it collects

her prized Batavia bicycle, old laptop,
her one enamelled Creuset pot. Praying

they won't be spotted, the winged spirits
of Viró's sculpture hover breathlessly

above, as he ransacks below for saleable goods.
Circuit complete, Paul pauses with his haul, props

the door ajar to thread his wobbly cart
back out. Wind leaks through the bedroom window,

imparting movement to Viró's spirits.
Hinged plaster wings flap reluctantly –

colliding pieces clink, sound varying tones
like a xylophone. Paul looks up, alarmed,

to find the chiming's source, or charm:
*What's that?*
he asks.
*Something I'm making. Made.*
*Well, shit.*

A bit unnerved, Paul stands on tiptoes,
lifts his hand to block a winged bull

with a six-eyed seagull's face. A cup fused
to its forehooves taps his raised palm.

The flying creature halts; transmits a shockwave
that makes the whole flock spasm

like a box of broken glass.
*Don't touch it,*
Viró pleads, *it's all balanced – it'll fall.*
Paul's

eyes flick from shape to shape, past droplets,
cups, blades, and sliced and spitting snakes and rats

that spin around a tree –
*My Dad collects.*
*He'd want to see this.* The shapes rebalance,

resume their dance. *It's ours now,* Paul declares,
*by law. Dad might forgive your rent arrears*

*for clear provenance, full copyright.*
*But it's ours. The exit cameras*

*will spot you if you sneak a piece out, we'll call*
*the cops. Act weird, we'll lock you out.*

*It's – wow, it's magnificent work,* Paul says
at last in a different voice. *What a thing.*

He leaves Viró wiping tears from her cheeks,
cracked fingertips streaking ashy-blue bangs

with blood. A gecko-laugh rattles in her
stick-thin neck. *Five days is impossible.*

She feels betrayed by Reddit, her own mistakes
and the beautiful thing she made.
How far

can you get without leaving the kingdom?
The lonely sidewalk east, the western

beaches? What do you reach if you dig
through asphalt matrices into the hackings

beneath of clockwork, wires, and pipes?
Weaving
their trucks through urban streets like Pacman sprites

through mazes, Adanac's staff fix leaks, mend
flood damage, restore hookups between

private and public pipes. Under sinks,
cracked valves and gaskets get replaced –

from toilet drains where toddlers live
plastic action figures are snaked. Skilled hands

rip out waterlogged baseboards and Gyprock
bloated by weeping, leaks, and overflows,

trim drywall sheets on their tailgates
to patch what they removed, stir

buckets of joint compound to wipe across cracks,
bury screw heads. Tracking progress

as crews check in between job sites,
Coral's gladdened by how Adanac's guys

are working fast to squeeze in the jobs Jas
would have done, racing from site to site, proud

to report each task they finish. Coral's
reminded of Adanac's early days,

when they'd come south with nothing but their camper,
Mark's tools, and hours in which to work.
Mark

glories in not needing a list to know
what jobs to hit: some trick of genetics

lets him learn Coral's schedules
at a glance – the names, details, and status

of each account. It's a faculty
that helps him also count cards, tempts him

to chance more than they can afford on odds
he fancies he can reckon better than the house.

Offering rebates for payments made in cash
Mark builds up piles of bills in his glovebox

to hazard in poker games he'll play
while Coral sleeps.
Suburban old folks

rinse breakfast dishes, raise condo blinds
to stare at the active city. Magnolias

droop waxy scoops; cherries are puffed with pink;
tulips poke Crayola tips through muddy soil.

Mehrdad wipes the Jackson Pollock petals
off his Buick's windshield with long fingers,

reparks across the street in case the scheduled
sweeper-truck comes this week. Too old to smell

his smeared palms, Mehrdad half recalls, half
reimagines the petals' whiff of white wine

gone stale, floral odours like the perfumes of
melting ice cream – flicks back to his wife's last days

when Armin wanted flowers wall to wall
filling vases, cups, then buckets to blot out

the miasma her dying flesh gave off.
*Never enough*, thinks Mehrdad, meaning both

flowers and days. Post-mortem, a collie bitch
borrowed from a chess buddy sat in

for the sagdid, panting by the bedside.
She licked his trembling hands

till crematoria workers trucked
Armin's mortal shell away. He walked the dog

home, and returned alone to rooms brim-full
of flowers, and Saena, Armin's canary,

singing pertly from perch to perch,
offensively alive.
                    Today, Mehrdad

expects his second grandchild to be born,
and he's on call to watch his son's one toddler

when an induction pill kicks in,
and Mary heads to the hospital to birth

a gastroschisic boy who may
or may not live. *But babies come at night,*

he thinks, *there's still all day to kill.*
Slapping tweed cap on his bald head,

still brackish from the whisky that helped
him fall asleep last night, Mehrdad strolls

mall-ward for chess, where he'll kibbitz, blitz
on food-court tables till his turn to compete

on the big board comes. Alekhine's Defence,
Closed Sicilian, Semi-Slav – he still

studies these and improvises endgames
with such automatic skill that when his mind is gone

his fingers will play on. At the mall he finds
a game gone static, Serb and Croat letting

their match wind down to a draw. Mohammed
and Dennis nod at Mehrdad. *Morning, gents,*

Mehrdad says, then asks Mo about Saena.
*Cheerful little chit, but misses you, no doubt.*

*Come visit anytime you like.*
                                                  Mo drops
his voice so only his friends can hear:

*We three – let's play at the beach today.*
They wander to the waterfront, resting

only by the pitch and putt to watch otters
glissade through a water hazard's sluices,

watch white petals blow off a row of plums.
At the outdoor chessboard laid in two-tone tiles,

they're peeved to find the pieces missing,
still stored for winter in a padlocked

pre-fab shed. Thirsty, the three old men buy juices
from a machine, and under specimen trees

where lacewings display for mates, take turns
sparring with city hall on Mo's cellphone and

jogging for the loo. A golf-cart buzzes up,
clicks on its brake. It brings a teen with a key

who lugs out sixteen statuettes in black
and sixteen white. It's hot before the first pawn's pushed.

Mo falls to Mehrdad via zugzwang; Mehrdad
gets forked, drops a rook to Dennis, resigns.

They refill plastic bottles at a fountain,
sit squeezed on a park bench to contemplate

the view. Concrete path. Sun-bleached driftwood logs.
Foraging crows half-hopping, half-gliding

between boulders. Tidal rip, the sea
a-sparkle.
                    *So much resides*, observes Mohammed,

*in the qualities of light.* Blonde yachts swan through
narrows below the bridge. Toddlers sweat

in parkas on the playground though cautious parents
keep them to the shade. Mehrdad's reminded

of his daughter-in-law Mary, how earnest
she looks when shepherding Larissa,

how carefully she's placed her feet
this pregnancy, afraid she'd lose the flawed foetus

if she tripped. *My son's expecting a boy,*
he says, as he lights a cigarillo,

aware it makes him look silly, but still
liking the taste. *His wife's being induced today –*

he exhales his first full breath of smoke,
and waves to ward off their congratulations –

*There's trouble. The belly – the abdomen didn't*
*seal. His guts are floating loose.*
                                                *Will he live?*

asks Dennis.
                        *If his organs still work, yes.*
*If not, likely no. They find out when he's born.*

*This, I will pray for,* offers Mo.
Dennis gulps *Me too*. Mehrdad learned

what prayers and hospitals were worth
while Armin wasted away for no cause

doctors could name or cure. But
what's it all for if not for this?
                                                Mehrdad

pats their knees in thanks.
                                    *Armin*
*would have asked better,* he thinks. *She was*

*perfect at times like these. Kind thoughts,*
*kind words, kind deeds.*
                                    Jogging girls flit past,

ponytails swishing side to side, and hounds
walked professionally in packs strain

in passing to warm the old men's hands.
*God is good*, pants Dennis, and Mohammed nods.

## MORNING SPENT

*Which god's the good one?* No one knows or wants
to know. An outbound cruise ship sounds its horn –

wakes Enoch with a lurch, thinking he's being called
to work. At school, his son's excused from French,

from flashcards for *chien* and *boeuf*, *rien* and *neuf*.
Thinking of his mother and the riddles

she unpacks in whispers for him alone,
Samson whisks outside before he nears

the bathroom door, ducks into a hollow
between blackberry canes and cinderblock wall.

There's a pickled smell in here, the smell
of secret doings behind a screen of leaves

where the revving bees drown out PA announcements
and urgent bells. Samson thinks of tinkling off

his dad's dinky sailboat as he muddies
the ground with piss, shakes off the drips, re-zips.

Vapours rise from the moistened plant debris
like mosquitoes, and he, missing the sea

and his mother's sweetness, gets lonely
and cold, worn Yonex soles squeaking

in the corridor as he returns.
Jack thanks
Connor for his winning spiel as they gloat

with cigars on O-Con's balcony. *Good work*,
Jack growls as his hands flap a plasticky applause,

*Great work. How'd it feel to break the hundred*
*million dollar mark?*
Connor grins. *Feels great,*

he says, watching the smoke drift up – *like*
*no gravity. You know, those suckers were so*

*hypnotized, I could see speck-sized reflections*
*of myself mirrored on their eyes. And you,*

*still want more before we jet?*
Jack groans:
*Connor, my whole life long, I get one shot*

*at catching a fish this big… we gotta reel it in.*
*I'm telling you, we "profit share" ten million,*

*those clucks will think we're gushing cashflow.*
*Picture the frenzy when we* IPO*!*

*Cash out then, we'll split another digit,*
*maybe take home a yard apiece.*
Connor nods,

chokes on a suck of smoke. Jack side-eyes
his ally, decides not to mention the hints

that Murray gave him when they met
earlier on the street, that they should spin

their profits into some goldmine scam he owned
or else… cinders sink like sediment

toward the lawnmower's stutter and drone
in the cloister below. But Jack turns the topic,

has sad, sad news – his mother's dying.
Jack's flying home (a week, he thinks), asks Connor

to pilot O-Con while he's gone. Connor
wishes Jack's family well. Jack pulls him in

for a bear-hug – his chest so wide Connor
feels dwarfed by the embrace, reminded of

his dad's hugs when he was small.
                                        Jack lets go,
blows a hula hoop of smoke, and winks:

*Got coffee at Arque today. Goddamn,*
*that girl of yours got eyes like a cartoon kitten.*

*Half the guys downtown would crush*
*either nut in a vice to fuck her once. Gonna get*

*that bunny on your boat outta here, put*
*a baby in that belly?*
                                *Maybe*, Connor says,

fingering the ring-box in his pocket.
*Fortune favours big dicks like ours,* Jack jokes,

a cellophane smile on his lips, *but don't forget:*
*girls are like buses – miss one...*
                                        Connor ends

Jack's maxim: *...the next's already on its way.*
*Don't rush your smoke,* Jack says, tossing his own

cigar off the railing as he goes,
*but I've got to tidy up before my flight.*

Connor frowns, dragging on his Cohiba
to keep its smoulder going. He finds Jack's fondness

for talking up their cocks obnoxious,
but without the fervour Jack exudes,

his own anxiety ramps up. Fear of getting caught
begins to pump through his capillaries,

warming his skin so quickly it burns. Lunch
with Vanessa looming, Connor clears his mind

by taking a drive: careening his hot hatch
around roads that perforate the park, past

taped-up gaps in the causeway's bike-lane barrier
where late-night Lambos bashed steel posts loose

when they crashed. Jack had promised him
the glory when he disclosed what O-Con was

(*Though it's dreams*, he said, *that make men rich)*
and proposed partnership, saying *So long*

*as I can be Jesting Pilate, you can be*
*the Son of God,* and sketching a path

to a Jubilee Day when bag-holders
would bid up scheduled dumps of stock before

Omniopticon went bust and he and Jack
would toss inculpatory laptops in the sea,

sail off on matching yachts to the Maldives.
*In Meradhoo*, Connor swears, *I'll buy a Porsche,*

as his Mazda weaves its route through woods
where flickers pick punky stumps apart

for sowbugs; milky salal roots tunnel
through the soil, while tar-black feelers

of bracken lift translucent claws from lawns.
In culverts he steers over, caddis larvae

tuck sextets of obsidian legs within barrels
of needles and bark – he veers past mats

of crushed moss where postpartum does
lick their kittenish fawns' fur clean, afterbirth

still steaming in the natal beds they've made.
In groins of maple trees whose leaves are stirred,

disturbed by the Mazda's trailing vortices,
liquorice ferns soak sweet flavours

from the sugary sap their roots suck; on alders,
identical ferns absorb a bitter taste

from their seats. We never hunt the cocky geese,
never harvest ducks or swans from ponds.

What's it all for, if not to forget the past,
build monuments to what we hope

will someday be?
Viró's popping by friends' porches
to borrow ten bucks here and twenty there.

She's cadging what she can, sensing
it won't be enough to prevent the sculpture

she spent months to make being taken
by her rapacious landlord. Shrill phrases

repeat like sirens in her head: *Five days?*
*Not near enough. But what else can I do?*

*Make a deal? Give that snake the gods, and rights*
*to replicate, revise my work? So that's*

*what artists do,* she tells herself. *Sell our works*
*to live. But not like this. I'd rather die.*

She takes laneways between friends' addresses,
shy to be seen astride the bike share Norco

she's forced to ride. She tries to ignore
its handlebar placard selling lime-flavoured lager

and plastic mud-guards covering half the wheels,
gaudy with ads for local casinos.

She thinks instead how Paul pawed
through her belongings, smooth face blatant

with distaste before, exultant when he saw
her art. *That's arrogance,* she thinks, *to hide*

*neither contempt nor covetise.* She regrets
not arguing to keep her Ladies' Batavia

at least – she could have said it was for work,
even if he'd countered the public six-speeds

were free to use. Friends are distressed
when Viró knocks on their kitchen doors

so wan: arms and legs gaunt as necks
of cormorants, fingertips crazed with pink cracks

as they gratefully pull from outstretched hands
the offered cash. At stop lights, she pings

binners who specialize in phones, asking
what they've got in hand, debating rates. None

will sell on credit and why should they?
It's day-to-day for them like it is for her:

*God's grace is one thing for the sparrow*
*on the feeder,* her father used to say,

*another for the falcon in the pine.*
Taste us. We taste of this place, no other,

though foreign sigils fly on the roofs
of office-blocks, flapping in the wind.

## NOON

Atop office blocks, winds flap patriotic
graphics, trickle liquified down sunlit ropes

to cloisters below. Across a grass plaza
wind rubs its palms, flips waves of green blades to grant

glimpses of zinc undersides,
sucks snakelike smoke from a cigar dropped burning

from above. Enoch crouches
at his easel, a paintbrush pinched crablike

between fingers and thumb. To pacify
the phantom waves his sea legs still hallucinate,

his boat shoes press on concrete pavers, while,
arthritic from strain and storm, he tries to make

his trembling brush-tip mimic this wind at work,
imitate not only the images his eyes perceive,

but shapes his mind knows underlie them.
Snow-white hairs lift on his cheek,

and a second life shivers in his thinning skin
as paint transcribes how waves of zinc

pass through uncut grass, how wind extracts
dark streaks from the discarded cigar.

A two-stroke mower has already shorn
half the membrane between earth and breeze

that attracted Enoch's eye, but the workman
flicks the engine off with a cough to fill

its tank with mix. Enoch's brush takes the chance
to catch up.
Enoch likes to leaf at night

through watercolours of wave and wind action
he painted in a prior life, while Anna swam

off their anchored boat, diving to lift
shellfish from the wild seafloor for supper.

Sometimes she surfaced with yelps of success
and sometimes she'd yell, a crab's pincer fixed

to her pointer, a pink puff in the chuck.
He's burnt most pictures he drew of her, though

still ruminates on why they failed – strife
between the chances for effect arising

whenever brush marks a blank with shape,
and the idealized likeness a lover

deserves to see.
He knows he repels her now,
but the miracle is that she ever felt otherwise

about the spider-silk of his body hair,
the wrinkling around his eyes.
Airhorns bray

an anthem's first few notes. All hierarchies
of labour cease: statisticians pause analyses

of per-user-hour spend on freemium games –
designers leave designs half-limned –

draft emails gleam unsent on a million screens
while workers on break run the seawall or read,

flip tractor tires to slog through sand
for exercise. Hungry queues watch pork sliced,

crackling diced, and salsa verde grease
both block and knife. Tanned C-suiters await

mentees in mock-trattoria, expensing
what field-tripping retirees order up

for treats while vertical ropes drip liquefaction
down the sky.
Foot plastered to the gas,

Mehrdad weaves his Buick through traffic:
Mary's plug dropped, and Yusuf needs his dad

to sit with Larissa while they go down
into the darkness to bring back a baby

or body. Yusuf's waiting by the door,
opens up before he knocks, hands him

a printed sheet with what to do and not to do,
though further explanations get cut off –

*Go! Go!* Mehrdad urges, holding the elevator open,
and they do, Mary kissing Larissa

as she goes, urging her *Be good for*
*Pedar Bozorg! We love you! We'll be back soon!*

But Larissa's watching Peppa Pig,
doesn't even twitch her head of lavish curls

except to dodge the kiss. Mehrdad
catches Mary's eyes skeptically assessing him

as she tilts around him to the lift,
hypersensitive nostrils flaring to check him

for a whiff of liquor. He smiles
as the sliding doors close.
                                        Mehrdad's

unsure what to do next: he's not sat Larissa
solo before this, since his strata forbids kids,

and he fears the two-year-old and he
share little, besides their eyes' lines and a liking

for zoolbia. Seeing she's at peace with the TV,
Mehrdad hangs his jacket and cap

beside an Esfand sconce. While the kettle boils,
he takes stock of pull-ups and wipes, scans

the whirring fridge for snacks Larissa likes,
roots through cupboards for booze –

concludes he'll need to buy a bottle. Tea
steeping in its pot, he skims Mary's list

of to-dos and do-nots. Most are tied
to meals or hygiene but a daunting set

itemize the Byzantine routine required
to coax Larissa to sleep. *Was it so hard*

*for Armin?*
            A divô's lit wick flickers
beside the sink, its reservoir of ghee

recently refilled. Mehrdad sighs, not shocked
his son wouldn't trust him to tend the sacred flame

as he peeks over the deck's railing
to check if his Buick's been ticketed.

Seeing no chit on the windshield, Mehrdad
settles on the rug beside Larissa, greeting

his granddaughter with a tap.
*Oh hello, Grandpa Bozo,*
Larissa replies with mild surprise,

then explains unasked, at length, non-stop,
who the cheerful creatures are onscreen

and what they want.
Her hearing adjourned
till two, Anna's walking desk-ward to type

reply notes, but halts – spotting Enoch
in the cloister between two towers,

straightening from his canvas. It startles her
to notice how much muscle he's lost,

how anthocyanin capillaries
pink and purple his leaf-thin skin. He stoops

for the discarded cigar, draws
on the tobacco quizzically – then puffs again,

impressed, to savour its acrid taste
before crushing it on a tree, dropping

it on the tree's cramped roots. Anna's heart sinks,
seeing him as the other citizens do:

a mislaid Robinson Crusoe, unfit
for the kingdom. *What must the school kids*

*think?* she frets, *when Samson's claimed*
*by this throwback, this scruffy flotsam*

*smelling of the sea?* She sighs. *At least he's free.*
Anna grips her briefcase tighter,

resumes her rush.
Enoch hears her high heels
clatter, be lost in the urban ambience.

He's glad to think she stopped to watch him,
even if not to wave hello.
Boeing droning

overhead, Meghan picks plush salmonberries
by an old railway, awaits a friend's friend

who moonlights as a healer.
Before
her first birthday, Meghan picked these berries:

Feng held her up so Meghan's moth-soft hands
could grab the red and yellow quilts of fruit,

stuff them in her infant mouth, and feed
some carefully to her mother's mouth, smiling

to see her mother smile. Feng remembers
those picnics each March to May, when khaki twigs

bloom violet, then berries swell from quilled
green lumps to amber and ruby hauberks

that glut the thrushes' and waxwings' beaks.
But Meghan's long-since shed those memories –

is tortured instead with disease-induced
delusions of how her nanny abused her,

rented her in her Pack 'n Play to pedophiles
while her dad was overseas, her mom

too overworked to see. She bites
a spoiled berry, and when she's spat it out,

stares with sympathy at a maimed white grub
writhing among seeds and juice.
                                                  The passing Boeing

pushes past ropes of sunlight before banking
over the sea to line up for the runway.

Low and slow, its cruciform shadow
flutters through shallow water; a grey,

Ash-Wednesday smudge haloed with a rainbow
only those onboard can see. Above the highway

entering town, a neon sign glows
with the message *God is Good! Believe!*

and the Pilot's Glory proclaims the same to fliers
pressed to plastic panes and looking down.

## LATE LUNCH

*The President's got plastic pains*, Glen groans,
long bare arms pushing his cart of cans

and salvaged gadgets through the complaining cone
of the afternoon. Starved for Seroquel,

he stomps past the courthouse bike racks, past hives
of shops who leak their scents of soaps and soups,

Top 40 tunes that can't drown out
the snake's persistent hiss, insisting still

on its disgust for life. Sweating beneath
the Bulls jersey he always wears, Glen senses

as cravings stir in the perfumed air
and sublimate unnoticed by others,

quarks that pop in and out of mental pores.
White-collar workers hear the frustrated

rattle of Glen's shopping cart over concrete
cracks and back away to let him pass,

as Dante saw dismal citizens give space
to a visitor who had no place there.

On café patios, flocks of starlings
peck crumbs from deserted plates, and as Glen

nears, his monologue morphs into a sermon
preached to the screeching birds: *This*, he intones,

*is not the place for us to be hypnotized!*
*Under hypnosis, it was Brooklyn who stole*

*your baby. She can't have one, she's had gangrene*
*from birth – she'd give your baby gangrene with her penis.*

That warning uttered, he reaches his garden,
parts the green lean-to tarp and whispers:

*Wake up, Brooklyn, and marry me! Come out!*
*Your mother and the President agree*

*it's time we leave the kingdom, time we got*
*some goodness for ourselves.*
He puts his head inside.

Empty. Nothing but light stained a submarine tint
by the green tarp's weave, his bottle of pills,

a rustling hiss. An embossed hose of snakeskin
lies where it was shucked. Noiseless files of ants

tote impedimenta through the tent. In one
bright aperture, a clutch of spiderlings

thins out – hatchlings consume weaker sisters
as they stilt-walk towards the sun.
Trading ends

in New York. Minor traders tally
PnLs, log off rigs to text colleagues,

make calls to clients in the hour of downtime
before futures bidding starts. Bored

in his cloud-high office, Murray's been
sucking sips from his tumbler of rye,

trading tips with allies out east – puffing stocks
he needs to dump, torching tickers

he wants to buy. At his age, Murray's never sure
which friends he's burned, and which

he's yet to scorch. He's tired all the time
and there's a sick taste on his tongue, an ache

in the dewlap that wobbles below his chin.
His phone jingles like a shaken coin purse –

one of his sons. He checks. It's a text
from Paul, an orthopaedic surgeon, who,

when not replacing knees, runs Murray's rentals
to please the old man. He's seized goods

from the deadbeat in K303, but reports
moreover she's an artist, has work

set up in the room Murray will want to see.
Murray swipes his phone screen blank.

*Paul's a philistine,* he thinks, *probably some*
*semi-abstracted vulva or a pickled cat,*

*some punk trash pretending to be smart.*
Work's never done, but he's done for the day.

Though he feels too ill to eat, he goes
to schmooze tables at the steakhouse he owns –

treats some soccer players to *caipirinhas*
in honour of their Brazilian rookie –

a deaf kid who smiles, sips the drink
he never liked, and nods his thanks. Murray bows,

spies Connor and intercepts him before he reaches
Vanessa's side.
*Hey kiddo,* calls Murray,

*how's your dad? I met your date when she came in,*
*she said you'd be coming.* Murray cups

his hairy hands to beckon the younger man
in closer, admiringly pokes his tie:

*Loved your pitch for O-Con, kiddo. Those guys buy?*
*Who could resist! Wish I had a penny*

*to pop in the pot, but mine's all tied up in mines.*
*My line's goldmines, kiddo – all kinds,* he adds,

lifting hirsute hands to embrace
the steakhouse. *But they're money pits*

*unless you time 'em.* Murray sidles closer,
smooths Connor's suit with a tailor's touch

as the young man fights to maintain a smile.
*X-A-U*, Murray spells out sotto voce,

his gullet jello-like with excitement.
*Next week's the assay news. Could be talking*

*Klondike-type bonanza, shoe-shine kiddos*
*at the airport getting rich on tips. Scoop*

*enough stock and we'll name the pit after you,*
*or* (cocking his head at Vanessa) *any chick*

*you'd like to wow. O-Con's a gem, but eggs and baskets.*
*Word to the wise: I don't read Chinese, but*

*an app on my cellphone tries. I took pics of* WIP
*on a few screens at your shop this morning:*

*bit of this, bit of that, but no* AI,
*no pattern-recognition shit. Wrong guy*

*sees those pics, could be bad for you and Jack –*
*so X-A-U on the venture exchange!*

*Tick tock, kid. Don't wait. I told Jack too. Borrow*
*if you have to. Best to your dad,*

*it's been too long. Tell him gimme a call,*
*we'll have a good time.* With that, Murray's gone,

his squat legs trotting smoothly through the crowd.
He's got other lapels to pluck, other ears

to hiss in. When Connor sits, he's shaken,
flushed. *Who was that?* Vanessa asks, *He tried*

*to buy me drinks while I waited.*
*A snake,*
says Connor (wanting to ask if she'd run,

if he ran), *who scammed my dad.*
*He died – my dad. I was ten. We lived*

*with Grandma after that.*
*I'm sorry,* Vanessa gulps,
guilty for how cut she'd felt, watching

Connor smirk awkwardly while the old shark
talked. *It's ok*, says Connor, ignoring

how the thin ice flexes beneath his feet,
the sounds it makes as cracks begin to spread.

*The game's the game. Snakes and ladders.*
*Climb way up, slide back down.*

*It could have been the other way round,*
*and maybe next time, he'll go down.*
From behind stacks

of store-brand muesli Larissa leaps,
screeching as lion-like as her treble lets her.

Mehrdad clucks with mock-alarm and ducks
for shelter from the pink and purple nails

she crooks into claws, from her flurry of curls
the colour of bread crust. Larissa shrieks

with joy, darts away to re-hide. Her grandad
laughs. This is all a new blessing for him

though he guesses Armin and Yusuf shared
similar games while Mehrdad juggled jobs,

kited cheques to bridge bad months. He's scored
a bottle of Pernod, and now he's killing

time – trolleying slowly along, trying
to please his tiny predator by naively

nearing her trap – but at the breakfast aisle's end
he's alarmed to find no ambush.
*Larissa?*

No tiny lion at the next turn either. His mind
eddies. He ditches their shopping cart

and lifts his old knees to a trot, trying not
to panic. His bald head jerks in search

of sound or motion, his lips repeat her name
with fervour as he checks ice-cream freezers,

aisles where juice and pop are stocked.
Lost?
Kidnapped?
He's heard of perverts grabbing girls

so young they forgot their mother's voice
before being found –
At customer service

he keeps his tone calm, explains what's transpired.
He's as ashamed as when he'd told legal aid

Armin wanted the charges dropped, but
*Happens!* Cheryl says from behind the counter,

summoning other staff by intercom.
*No fuss for us, it happens all the time.*

It's not true, but Mehrdad sees the lie
is kindly meant.
*Aisle six where you saw her last?*

They look under kiosks of cut flowers, in nooks
behind make-your-own-cupcake displays,

fruit crates, through cupboards in the closed café.
Then Cheryl's walkie-talkie crackles with news –

they rush back to the breakfast aisle,
where a teenage worker grins, bends down

to the lowest shelf, points into a gap
between boxes and Larissa asleep

in the sweet-smelling darkness behind. Mehrdad
breathes deep, so relieved he can hardly

stand straight as he offers Cheryl and
this grinning youth his thanks.
Huts

deep in the park house colonies of hermits
with their own economies of holiness.

*All's secret,* these anchorites preach – *all's*
*on sale in the kingdom and secret, so long*

*as the blind sea and sightless peaks bless us*
*without ceasing.*
Over campfires and

psilocybin they debate the same topics
hour by hour: *What are we? What answers*

*our gazes in mirror-mazes or from*
*surfaces of ponds? Are all our selves mirages,*

*false oases tricking a tribe lost*
*among arid atoms and abstract energies?*

*If not, what are we? To what do we belong?*
Adhering to diverse creeds, hermits push

pet theories, refute more than they can prove.
Sun's zenith past, disputants part ways

with the matter unresolved, wipe their palms clean
on shaded lawns still wet with last night's rain.

## SECOND HOUR OF AFTERNOON

On lawns still wet from last night's rain,
the kingdom of the clock's new moms push prams

past tennis courts where balls clip-clop from racket
to racket – sit on stumps with babies cupped

to breasts. Told at intake to walk a while,
Mary waddles painfully along the seawall

with Yusuf hand in hand. They trade *I'm-fines*,
and *How-are-yous,* discuss the weather and whether

Mehrdad will bother to read the guidelines
Mary's fretted over and refined. Mary

doesn't say she wishes her own parents were there –
that she envies those families where grannies

wake early to wrangle toddlers, ferry
older kids to sports and spelling bees.

But Mary's mother's out of reach: Mary
crossed the sea for Yusuf

who hovers,

watching to catch her if she trips. Feeling
as mortal as sailors riding out a storm,

they don't discuss the snakes of escaped
intestines they traced on ultrasound screens,

the outlines of foetal organs fallen
from the unborn baby's rift that a doctor

pointed to and explained. They're hoping
for fragility and pain instead of death,

praying those vagrant body parts will be ready
to be tentatively set in place

when the boy is born, and not tarry, putrescent,
leaving their child unable to live from day to day,

and no one to blame, if not themselves.
They do not guess how many citizens

who stroll beside them on the seawall
are rubbing from wrists and necks

the gluey residue of guilt –
                                        parents
whose newborn coughed up in its car seat,

inhaled the puke and died without a cry
while they drove home, carolling along

to classic rock –
                          a teen who flipped
his grandad's truck into a pond, was saved

by strangers who held his stoned head above
the surface, while unnoticed in the seat

beside him, the boyfriend he'd kept secret
drowned –
               a widower who found one morning

that his son had been swapped for a cadaver
by an undetected heart flaw while he slept –

many know how close the knife carves to the bone,
how guilt polices them, like wasps that nest

beneath the eaves, but they keep their knowledge
secret – a matter between themselves and ghosts

that orbit above, bearing blades and empty cups.
Around the city, small lives drowse,

digest, and squall in queues while mothers
duck dirty looks, rock back and forth. These matrons

are served in coffee shops by single girls
in silks and leggings, uncaught as sprites of streams

and woods. Now that bright smiles and blackened lashes
behind tills are for their benefit, mothers

recognize the same *joie de jour*, the same
gaits and manners they once deployed for pay

in hotel foyers and chic cafés before
they bore babies. Such playacting behind them now,

mothers trot the seawall, touched to the hipbone
by the sight of Mary and Yusuf in limbo,

while anchorites peer out from rhododendrons
to eye the solemn couple as if witnessing

a groom and goddess of the corn
or king's son and daughter bringing garlands

for a fatted bull in some sacrificial rite.
Not guessing that Mary's waiting to discover

whether a runaway train will take the fork
that cuts her hopes apart, these prophets

see Mary's beauty and its ripening fruit
like every birth as splicing mortal

with immortal – sanctifying imperfect
flesh, and wedding it back to lonely souls

still dancing cell to cell.
Mark inspects
some flood fix-up at a west-end mansion,

asking Inez (the housekeeper who hired
Adanac) how her Chow Chow reacted

to the racket. She says Diez tracked Jas
while he worked, yipping and yapping

for the treats the man kept in his tool belt.
Mark's beard crinkles with pleasure:

it was his idea to arm the guys with doggie treats.
He asks after her daughter in Cuba

she'd said was sick when he did her estimate.
Inez says the toddler's better now, but

it's torture to be apart when her babies
are sick. Does he have kids?
*Not yet*, he says,

not wanting to get into it, *the time's*
*not been right.* His glance flicks towards Inez

and the skin under his beard reddens.
He bends back to examine the baseboards,

afraid he's made a gaffe: she's what –
twenty-two? And has two kids already? Three?

*Sorry,* he says. *Waiting for all the bits*
*to fall in place probably isn't a game*

*you got to play.*
*There is no right time,*
Inez sighs, *just God's time. Trust me, I know.*

Her mention of God makes Mark's blushes
blush.
*Jas did good,* says Mark, but he's got

to cut the chit-chat short, hit his next stop.
Pocketing the cash she hands him, he thanks

Inez, adds, as he walks out to his truck,
*God Bless!* with cadences he'd polished

growing up in church. There's a text
from his wife: *Think we should thank the boys?*

*Pick a bar tonight for drinks?* Mark grins;
he knows she prefers places playing songs

they know, cheap chilled pitchers of beer, hot meat
platters meant to sate the appetites

of working men, but as Adanac's grown,
Mark's own yen has turned to joints where

moustachioed mixologists twirl test tubes
under coloured lights, decant elixirs with

eyedroppers. She's letting him choose as a special treat.
He'll be magnanimous, he decides,

and compromise, pick a spot with class, but not
what she'd call flash.
At Omniopticon,

Connor finds his monitor blank, his laptop
missing, and orphaned cords forlornly

tangled on the floor. The CEO's office
is empty too – Jack's computer gone,

empty desk drawers ajar. Connor totters.
Sweat slithers down his back, his tie knot's

suddenly too tight. He checks the O-Con
bank account on his phone – finds the balance

shrunk from a serpentine of nine figures
to a fish-head four. The walls and furniture

whirl in Connor's head as if O-Con's offices
were swirling down the drain.
*No, no,*

he thinks. *Jack wanted to go big or go bust,*
*shoot for a boffo IPO before*

*we cash a penny out. Jack wouldn't ditch,*
*leave me marooned, alone.*
Connor knows

he's playing with Potemkin hopes, knows
Jack's betrayed him, swapped their cash for crypto

and vanished down some bolt-hole. He's not
denying truth when he says it isn't so –

instead, he's praying for time's arrow
to undo its flight, the way he reverts

to save states in an arcade game, replays
till he beats it.
*Is this game still winnable, or done?*

There's no Jack left to turn in when cops knock,
no bargains to make, no funds with which to run –

but the illusion of O-Con's unbroken,
four floors of plexiglass desks are still filled

with workers improvising pantomimes
as persuasively as before, shoulders still

discreetly shielding symmetrical secrets
from the rest.
At the airport, Jack boards

a departing flight for Thailand,
where he owns a beachfront home

he's never mentioned in the kingdom. Already
he's called and woken Kittisak, his

long-time local agent, told him
to drive up from Tonsai Beach and when

Bangkok's banks open convert what he finds
in Jack's crypto wallet into kilos

of physical gold – hire guards with guns,
hydraulic dolly, and armoured car

to cart the boxed trove safely to branches
of ICBC and Cathay United, to be

transformed again into brokerage accounts,
portfolios of irreproachable

blue chip equities and bonds.
                                        His plane
taxis, lifts off, and begins to climb. Cityscapes

beyond Jack's oval window slip back
to show their sprawl, are smoothly replaced

by endless ocean and a blue horizon
gently bowed.
                    Jack always knew that someday

he'd say goodbye to the kingdom, shift
his winnings through the blockchain

overseas. Now he's torn between regret
at leaving O-Con so early in the scam,

and the thrill of being reborn. Obeying
his chameleon's instincts, Jack begins

to imagine his future as a wealthy expat,
a benefactor of local hospitals and schools,

a big fish in a backwater. He thinks with a pang
of his first Thai lover, who he'd lost

to cystic fibrosis when lung transplants
didn't take. He fondly imagines funding

research into transplant technology,
making a difference to someone else

while living out his days unsung, watching
the waves wash slowly in.

## Southbound

at the casino stop, train-cars release
sad crowds of gamblers, but before

the sliding doors bump shut, a crow
glides in from the platform. A lurch:

they're off again through hackings beneath
the kingdom of the clock, as the frantic bird

clatters from window to window, scratching
plexiglass before its trajectory ends

on the shuddering floor. Seeing the crow
wields a steak-knife in its beak,

passengers laugh, cameras click. Online,
the corvid's wild stare, the keratin-clamped

serrated blade go viral, get memed, pop up
in newsfeeds before the black shape

flaps out at the next stop, lights doubled
on plexiglass like the shells of wobbling moons.

## END OF SCHOOL

Inflexible metal bells like mottled moons
in school hallways hang silent until the pre-wired time

when steel tongues rattle the raucous shells,
free teachers from restless ears and eyes, free kids

to horse around in the schoolyard, leap into
parents' SUVs. Samson's dad arrives

on foot, toting his folding easel and paints.
*You're always late,* shouts Samson and runs

to thump into Enoch with a hug. They turn
to walk, Enoch watching, with a pang, how

the other, younger parents all seem to match.
Enoch's free hand rubs the fur of his son's nape.

*At least,* he thinks, *I've lasted long enough*
*he'll remember me.*
Cracked fingertips wrapped

in Band-Aids pilfered from the café's kit,
Viró helps Vanessa flip rattan chairs onto tabletops,

wipe flasks and filters clean. The two of them
close up while Viró explains her crisis,

how her landlord's trying to steal the sculpture
she's taken months to make. *How much*

*do you owe?* asks Vanessa, then, shocked: *How much*
*is your rent?* When Viró tells, Vanessa's

outraged: *Why didn't you join us at the Manor?*
*My rent's a quarter yours.*
Viró doesn't want to say

*I couldn't very well go on fooling*
*myself over you, staying up in hopes*

*you'd drift home alone…*
instead cites her public
rationale:
*We're too old for communes,* and
asks accusingly: *How many share*

*your Manor, Nessy?*
*Nine, if you count Callum,*
Vanessa concedes. *There's an empty room.*

*But only four or five are home most nights.*
Viró shrugs, runs fingers through her flimsy

blue hair as if to check how fast it's falling out.
*Maybe so. But I owe what I owe. How much*

*can you spare?*
Her ask vibrates in the air
as Vanessa thinks of her first year

in the kingdom, how Viró (living then
under a different name) met her on a film set:

Both needed a roommate, and for a season,
they were inseparable, joined at the hip.

But Vanessa grew wary of Viró,
not liking how her friend pressed against her

on the couch, how at strange times Viró's face
would shine. She thinks of scoffing *I take care*

*of myself – why can't you?* but feels pity
for Viró's deluge of imperatives

and respect for her reckless obedience
to art.
Vanessa laughs: *Connor always pays,*

*so you could say I'm rich these days.* She dips
ten twenties from the till, dings her card

for the missing sum. *How is your Beau Big*,
asks Viró, accepting the folded bills,

enfolding her friend in a hug. *Bigger*
*every day*, says Vanessa, and compares

the meals Connor buys with the cheap fare prepared
at the Manor where windows rattle

when the dryer runs; his loft's panoramic
views with the tiny square of frosted glass

that funnels light into her room.
*Le Crocodile*
*tonight*, Vanessa says.
*Special occasion?*
*Honestly,*

*I think he's proposing. Just a vibe I get.*
*Yes?* Viró inquires.
While Vanessa ponders

what to say about her future, one chair
falls off its tabletop, recoils off

flexible legs like springs, bangs its backrest
on flooring like a bell's knocker.
*I guess,*

Vanessa grants.
                                    *Then I'm the first,* says Viró,
with a twinge in her long-limping heart, *to wish*

*you happiness.*
                                    Vanessa's phone pings;
the screen fills up with congratulatory texts

from actor friends – she's confused –
but finds: voilá, a voicemail from the Fringe.

They laud the script she's given up on, say
they've picked her play

to headline the fest: it's announced
already, and Vanessa, who'd not thought

of the Fringe since she clicked "Submit," begins
to shriek, the last to hear her own big news.

She pirouettes between the chairs, stops
to catch one that's begun to slip. Viró's glum

with her own urgency. *I gotta go,* she says,
*I'm glad for you, Nessy, but I'm running out of time.*

*I hope,* Vanessa wishes, *you get*
*that sweet Batavia back.*
                                                  The friends part

with hugs, trade offers of help. Viró zips
east on her dorky borrowed bike, her blood

pumping with joy to find Vanessa
no more the fierce sun that once scorched her

day by day, but not inert either: a glowing
satellite on which she can safely gaze.

Vanessa skips south to the waterfront
to feast her eyes on the wheat-like waves –

slips off her Vans to walk the wet sand
discalced. Prostrate waves adore her soles,

their chill labia licking gooseflesh up her legs.
She hums country songs from home about love

"stronger than the storm clouds clashing far
above the hill," worries why she doesn't feel

like that, and maybe never will.
Enoch

and Samson watch crows pick through ficus tide rows

for tidbits. The sand's bleachers of stranded logs
are occupied by off-work ESL

instructors passing flasks from fist to fist,
ogling Vanessa as she treads the ocean's lip

with lilac flats dangling from pink fingertips.
Jeans rolled up, father and son footrace

in the greasy surf like Achaeans, skip
stones like little boys. When driftwood floating

in the shallows is revealed as a dead seal,
Samson's appalled, but Enoch rolls the corpse

by onc rubbery flipper until he sees
red seeping through the silver pelt.

*See this?* Enoch says, pointing at the bullet hole,
*Some fishing boats still carry shark rifles*

*to cull seals, afraid they'll steal salmon, rip*
*expensive nets.*
Moved by pity, Samson rests

his palms on the fur and tests the whiskers
on its upper lip with childish fingers.

Enoch nods his approval, recites words
he lived by long ago:
                                        *Most would rather*

*judge by sight than by the touch; for everyone*
*may look, but few may touch and feel; all can*

*perceive an appearance; few can grasp*
*what really is.*
                    Samson is agog: his father

never speaks like this to him.
                                        Watching
father and son from the tideline where she

stands, Vanessa's eyes sting with a need
for meaning and she gasps when they stroke

the seal as sad children stroke dying dogs
goodbye while a vet preps phenobarbital

for a lethal dose. Soft saltchuck pulsing
around the trio and her own fingerprints

prickling like battery contacts in a charger,
Vanessa rethinks energy and transformation

in her play, wonders if Viró can devise
special effects – clouds, flames, winged things

unfolding into being when a flap is flipped
like pages in a pop-up book.
                                        Enoch and Samson

solemnly strip to skivvies, wade into surf
with the buoyant body towed between them,

then swim side-stroke until the tidal rip
accepts their gift, drags it from their grips.

The water transmits Enoch's homily to the shore
as they swim back:
*Going to the sea…*

*The neatest, cleanest funeral in the world,*
*except it's free. When it's my time, I hope*

*you wrap me up with stones to help me sink,*
*send me down to the crabs to pay my debts*

*for all I've taken out by line and net.*
Vanessa makes a mental note of the old man's words,

and again, as man and little boy
huff and puff in the shallows, stumble

and shiver up the sand, she notes the schematic
of muscle and bone they share, one version

waning and one waxing.
ESL
instructors turn their smiling heads as absorbed

Vanessa passes by, bare feet pressing
resistant sand, her dancer's hips aligning

every stride. While grappa works in their veins
and sunlight warms their skins, two teachers

debate rival readings of Machiavelli:
*With more facility*, quotes one, *is a city*

*kept by her own Citizens, which hath been*
*us'd before to live free, than by any*

*other way of keeping.*
*Whoever,* his friend
quotes back, *becomes master of a kingdom*

*us'd to live free, and dismantells it not: let him*
*look to be ruin'd by it: for unless*

*the inhabitants be dispers'd,*
*the name of liberty is not forgotten,*

*nor its ancient order –*
but here they grow sheepish,
glance at the band's reserve across the water

where mobile homes and RVs mingle with
Tyvek-wrapped wooden frames; full-ton pickups;

driveways where kids shoot hoops, play Donkey
or Twenty-one. Along their river's lips,

a few tiny figures still flick fishing lines
from sandbars – waiting for rainfall, spate,

the salmon to run. A fenced gas plant
hums, vents flame to warp crossing sunrays.

Behind the plant, empty chip cars
trundle east, rumbling on seaside rails.

## MID-AFTERNOON

Chip cars rumble east on seaside rails,
shaking the creosote sheens of puddles coddled

between sleepers. Clanking over the truss bridge,
the train sheds droplets infused with soot

and industrial dust as Virò shoots
alongside – zig-zagging from friend to friend,

she grabs what scraps of cash they'll lend,
then races to the refundables co-op to rack

the Norco, loop cables to lock wheels front and back.
When binners trickle in with the day's finds

she's sweaty but smiling, the first buyer there.
She offends a few sellers by being choosy,

taking only items she can flip quick
and when rival buyers arrive, she despairs,

spares two-fifty for a demi of Rolled Golds,
ignites a contraband dart. She tries to charm

some binners into deferred payment terms
but they pluck at her ash-blue hair with palms

and fingers sticky with stale fermentations,
demand payment in kind in the alley

behind. Viró shakes her head, laughs it off
like it's something she knew they'd say.

She's going to cry and wants to explain:
*If you don't let me pay next week, I'll need*

*to steal so many phones – I don't even*
*think I can.*
But what's it all for,

if urban life doesn't free us from decay,
from dirt caressed into the skin's creases,

the stink of corn syrup gone sour
in sun-cooked cans, the sound of fish guts ripped

from between filets?
Enoch's smelled and shared
the panic of steers in the abattoir's hour,

of living fish brought flapping onboard, heard
the cough of the roman-nosed stag

with a bullet in his heart. He's worked
trawlers and ranches but never tells Samson

stories from those days, though Anna
wishes he would. Enoch wants his son's hands

clean, doesn't want him to butcher beasts,
scale fish, shoot quail or stand on their wings

to pull the best meat fresh from feathered,
still-warm sheaths.
Downtown, father and son

sit in moist clothes, sketching an alley where
a snarl of wires divides, filaments slip

through holes in brickwork. Eyes on his pad,
Samson tells Enoch about his day, about peeing

in the bramble patch. Enoch laughs, so pleased
to be told something clandestine by his son.

Wishing his dad in turn would tell him
something new, Samson gets tired of drawing

the mares' nest of wires his father likes,
turns to Art Deco motifs on old buildings,

the abstract facade of the new opera parkade
where there's a ruckus – a yearling bear

scrambling atop a garbage truck as if
it were a stump, frightened from a dumpster

when hydraulic prongs began to lift.
Phone in hand, Samson films as fire crews

arrive, then wildlife control.
A syringe-tipped pole hits the bear's rump –

the beast goes limp, slumps sideways
into a spread net. Cheers blare. Samson's video clips

go viral as quick as he shares them.
*What's it all for,* he thinks, *if not mercy?*

Enoch's work phone fizzles on his hip,
he swipes to take the Harbourmaster's call:

*Yes?*
        *Enoch, we've got –*
                                        *I'm off-duty, Rick,*
*I'm with my son.*
                                *Bring him. Johnny was taking out*

*an Aframax but collapsed. He's been choppered*
*to a doctor but the tanker's stuck – you know*

*she can't navigate without a pilot, it's the law.*
*She's dropped anchor near the sulphur terminal,*

*and tugs are holding her off the shore, but*
*she's full –*
                    *I'm coming,* Enoch says. He dials

Anna, but it goes to voicemail.
                                        *Love*, he says
without thinking, *there's half-a-million barrels*

*of crude oil stuck in the inner harbour.*
*It's a federal offence for them to sail*

*without a pilot. They need me, they're one*
*bad bump from a spill. I'm taking Sam –*
                                                  shoves

the phone back in his pants. Samson marvels
at how, with folding easel and paint-case

pinned in his left armpit, his white-haired dad
sprints as if his legs were springs, his free hand

gripping Samson's wrist to swing him across
a street as a light clicks green, traffic starts to flow –

how at the waterfront, he steps briskly
down steel rungs, leaps on a bucking prow

without a pause. Samson imitates
as best he can; hesitates, warm with pride

when his dad dismisses the driver's outcry
over Samson not wearing a PFD,

says Samson could swim home through any sea.
Twin Yamahas fold the wash into wings

until they stop alongside an oil tanker
four tugboats surround. A growl of reversed

props, a gyre of froth – they hop hand in hand
to a rope-suspended ramp.
                                        Halfway up

ringing, pendulous aluminium stairs
the skipper greets them; a spindly Brahmin

who leads them to the wheelhouse where they're welcomed
with applause. Enoch takes conduct, thanks

the Sikh bridge-team with handshakes,
explains the presence of his son. That done,

he takes stock, radios back to shore
with call-sign acrophony:
                                        *Harbour,*

*this is Lima-Whisky-Bravo-Xray.*
*Please advise when the narrows are open,*

*so we can untether the tugs. I'm hoping*
*to leave while the tide's still slack.*
                                                *Channel's yours,*

*Enoch, glad to hear your voice.*
                                                Samson's in awe
as his father instructs the tugs to cast off,

directs the orange-overalled Sikh helmsman,
the other officers manning controls, erect

and whiskered as Victorian cavalry.
A long horn blast thrills the air, the humming

deckplate moans when forward screws
engage. At main observation, facing out,

Samson and Enoch stand side by side, each
crossing his wrists behind his back. Officers

trade smiles when the little boy's right fingers
start tapping his soft left palm

in time to the rhythm of his dad's.
The main engine's tree-trunk-sized driveshaft

turns; vanes churn like whale-flukes. Samson's vantage
on the shoreline shifts; inner-ear otoliths

detect the vessel drifting west.
The suspension bridge connecting downtown

to northern suburbs grows closer: but
as they glide beneath its arc, Samson's world

shrinks till he could toss a stone
onto the paved seawall path to the south. Pigeons

roosting on I-beams of pillar and main deck
flap from their ledges, forming a kalakala

that flashes in clattering ellipses past
the ship's windows until the Aframax

eases into the wider world beyond,
reaching the open sea.
Trudging from court

with phone still silenced in her coat Anna
feels sick, her sense-organs disordered

by Justice Pomeroy's scowl,
the smug tone of the opposing lawyer

when he produced a transcript to prove
she'd finessed the truth too far, had "misled" –

What harm, when the clients on both sides
do nothing but lie? *Ah, never again,*

the old judge had said, in his Trinidadian drawl:
*All you have is your repute, and that can survive*

*one sin, but not a second.*
She thinks of the card
in her purse, and what she wrote it for.

*Only a few hours*, she thinks, *before I forgot*
*what I felt, fell back into pointless combat.*

*So what was it for?*
What should she do,
Anna wonders, give up the law? Then what?

Sail off in search of virgin soil, fulfill
Enoch's old fantasy of living off the land?

What about Samson's future? What about
her own? She can't flake out like Enoch,

who vanishes for weeks at a time
without warning, leaves Samson confused

and Anna scrambling for after-school activities
and babysitters. Enoch was always

frightened of the future, but she's starving for it –
when her stomach budded with the sparks

of Samson, she felt like the summer sun
had leaped into the sky
but he got spooked:

the needs he had to meet were suddenly
too great for Enoch's aging frame, his dwindling

stock of time. *Which leaves me,* thinks Anna,
*to be twice as steady and safe.*
Slouching

from courtrooms, the kingdom's barristers sigh
*O triple-booked gods who drowned the cities*

*once in inky seas: help us postpone*
*the unavoidable, ignore the unpleasant.*

*Let us not be startled or amazed*
*or show it, but help us hit deadlines,*

*make budget on our billables, collect*
*our fees without a fight.*
                                        Shuttering its eyes

to pray, the clock's metropolis goes blind
to true proofs of life's survival it longs

to see:
        seal dams nursing pups; an otter
sneaking down back alleys; the finned crescents

of dolphins and baleen whales
sunk in reflective waves like submarines.

Who has time to wait and watch in hope?
*Check online,* the signposts say, *for the virtual*

*vacation you deserve, for the chance to watch*
*proxies amass wealth and fame, wed to applause*

*of families and friends, make love, fawn over*
*smiling babies, watch sunsets from the beach.*

## LAST HOUR OF THE WORKDAY

Smiling babies, sunsets, beach-scenes,
parasailing clips pop up in feeds at five o'clock

as workers scroll through social apps. Killing
time till O-Con's workers leave and he

can lock up, Connor sits in a bathroom stall,
prays for clogged bowels to unblock

and tries to plot contingencies ahead.
*If Jack*
*calls the cops from overseas*, he tells himself,

*act dumb. Do nothing. If not, my best shot*
*might be to sell one final block of shares,*

*skip town with whatever they'll fetch. But who'll buy?*
*Jack had all the big-fish friends.* He imagines

begging the snake who'd once slipped a death wish
in his father's ear for one more slate

of suckers to pitch but *No,* he thinks,
*that won't fly, O-Con owes Murray fat fees,*

*and hasn't a penny to pay – he'd rat*
*in a flash if he guessed the golden goose*

*is out of eggs to lay.*
Unlike Emma Bovary,
modern-day Madame Bs like Connor don't dream

of being in romantic poems – only
the euphoric poses of perfume ads

could sate the insecurities he's fattened up
on the oblivion the kingdom gives:

a freedom from being known, from knowing
the neighbours we see parking their coupé

have just left the funeral of a young girl
who gobbled pills, fell asleep in the glass

coffin of a warm tub – from knowing they shook
the middle-aged hand of a man in sports coat and bad tie

whose fatherhood had been torn from him
the way deer break buds, leaves, branches

from orchard trees before the first fruit falls,
how they watched a newly-childless woman, helpless

as a ghost, ascend a pulpit to thank the crowd
for coming.
                    The kingdom's greatest gift

is to hide how quick the snake strikes, how fast
its venom acts. The clock's forward tick-tock

invites us to imagine every morning
that we're immortal, to mythologize

our daily lives, base tales of connection
on brief contact, or nothing at all.

In the real world, Connor can't decide –
he doesn't want to be like apes trapped

in a lion's cave who lie down, hands
across their eyes till they feel the lion's teeth,

but can't find a viable choice to free himself
from paralysis. He taps the hookup app

he swore he'd delete, swipes curated shots
to hot and not. *Please allow me to denounce myself,*

he DMs a match, *I'm a man of wealth*
*and taste.*

Clearing his head after court,
Justice Hugh Pomeroy lets the park's soft sun

evoke sensory echoes of his boyhood
spent in Trinidad seventy springs before.

Springtime wakes in his veins – and as he
once flayed waves with driftwood swords

to fend off imaginary hordes,
he swings his orthopaedic walking stick

at bracken shoots grown green and thick
beside the path. Cutting *tondo* and *fendete*

he enjoys each stroke, loves how sap sprays
when each severed fiddlehead drops.

Into his happiness, the calls of cops
intrude –

three police whizz up on bikes, dismount.

One yells: *Put your hands in the air.*

Hugh scoffs:
*For chopping weeds? Is this a joke?* but sees

handcuffs bared and tactical batons drawn.
By their smooth, not yet worked-in boots,

he can tell the trio are new recruits:
hyped up, amped, panting for a chance

to play with their newfound power.
His heart quails. He stiffens, so as not

to shake.
*Ah – this is wrong, all wrong,* he says,
*I'm not whoever you're looking for, I'm –*

*Drop the stick,* the spokesman barks, popping
his holster's strap – *Hands where we can see them.*

More words might make things worse, he knows,
and lobs his cane among the slaughtered ferns.

One cop manoeuvres behind him, crosses
Hugh's hands in the small of his back; Hugh cranes

his neck to watch with pangs of chagrin as pairs
of steel fangs click closed on his wrists –
surprised

at how umber his oft-forgotten skin
looks in the pink policeman's grip. Crows soar by.

Runners slow to gawk. Tour groups whisper, snap
cameras on their way past the scene

of black culprit and cops who strut and preen,
proud as any pack who've pulled their quarry down.

Their leader fishes out Hugh's wallet, reads aloud
his name with disbelief:
*Hughbert Elwyn*

*Pomeroy? And I'm Darth Vader, pal.*
*Where'd you score this fake ID?*
Hugh's bald scalp

twitches, but he holds his tongue.
*Give my name,*
Hugh says, when they call the collar in,
*tell them*

*who you've cuffed.*
The cops only relay
"the suspect is detained." *Google my name, then!*

Hugh insists. *Google my name if you feel*
*it can't go with my face.*
One cop, sensing

something's off, pulls out her phone, taps –
goes pale when the search results pop up.

*Ah, yes, now you see,* Hugh says.
*Aw, no, no, no,*
the cop patting his pockets says, finding

a courthouse ID with sober square photo
of Hugh in judicial robes.
*He's a judge –*

*let him go,* the cop on Google says,
lifting her phone aloft like holy writ.

*Don't you wish,* Hugh seethes, *you'd asked for ID first?*
The cops explain: *A Black male attacked*

*families by the beach. The description matched.*
*Can't you let it go? We are so sorry.*

*Ah,* Hugh growls, *imploring me not to make a fuss*
*while I'm still in cuffs, is, if I may say,*

*ill-judged.*
Fingernails scratch his wrists – the cuff's steel
teeth unclench. He stretches, smoothes out his sleeves

like a conjurer trying to recall
what's hidden up them.
Painfully, he bends

towards his dropped stick – until an officer
lunges to pluck it up for him.
                                        *If it makes you feel*

*better,* the cop offers, *they said a Black male in his forties.*
Hugh stares back at the trio of fools. *Worse luck*

*for you. Though it wasn't just your fault,* he allows
the woebegone cops, now more curs than wolves:

*No one senior enough to know me*
*wanted bike duty. Afraid of rain, were they?*

The cops titter.
                        *You still hope I'll let this go.*
*But this – this nonsense can't go on,* Hugh says,

though he knows it will, that it's a zombie
no one knows how to kill.
                                    *I'll have to make*

*a stink. But I'll tell them not to fire you three…*
*Since – Ah – once bit, they say, twice shy.* Hugh smiles

to let the officers blurt their thanks, then
ends: *Not that I'd want to be in your shoes,*

*acting contrite in endless interviews;*
*slews of new sensitivity courses*

*holding you up as "What-Not-To-Dos"…*
*while superiors grovel on the evening news.*

Abashed, confused, the cops
remount their bicycles and ride away, silent

except for the snap and rattle when each
nervously shifts gears.
                                Through air grown almost

gelatinized, a bald eagle flies past, mobbed
by crows that dive-bomb and torment

the pied raptor, who's too slow, too cumbered
with its own strength to catch or claw

its cawing attackers. Hugh watches the one-sided
aerial combat, admires the eagle's patience.

He knows eagles sometimes earn these assaults
by robbing nests of eggs or fledglings; and

sometimes crows, nest-thieves themselves, mob
eagles for sport or spite. Which it is today

he cannot say.
Glen cashes his day's cans
at the co-op; goes to display his scavenged

gadgets to the blue-haired girl who looks
more desperate than the other buyers,

a king-sized cig smouldering in her lips.
Viró looks through his collection, flips

her sky-dyed hair, annoyed – he's got
the scarce Huaweis she wants, but can't afford.

Hopelessly, she offers twice his price if he
can wait a week. Glen's thick lashes blink.

He shoves the slim black bricks at her
as if they held unforgivable sins,

refuses the IOU she offers in exchange.
*Ask the ants*, he says, *about labouring*

*for little sisters.* Viró says *Thank you!*
shouts *Thank you!* as Glen retreats, feeling

like a fraud. Viró ticks the items off her list, but
it's not enough. She needs more gear, much more,

though her store of borrowed cash is spent.
*The clock is running out,* she tells herself.

*No choices left but giving up or theft. Tick tock!*
*It's time to glean the fields.*
Cash in his pocket,

Glen parks his carts in a secret spot, struts
through a liquor shop's sliding doors

in celebratory mood.
Switches flick;
wheels spin. Legal fictions snap into being,

flush digital income through Forex
fly-by-nights before dissolving, assigning

debts to other spectres who use fluorescence
to lure the living near, mine data

from citizens' devices, spawn VOIP bots
who recite their tricks to voicemail boxes,

threaten charges for imaginary tax fraud,
and if payment terms aren't met, arrest.

Day spent, firms' tired receptionists
flick phone lines to voicemail, hook

wrists through handbag loops and scoot, hoping
to drop by the band store for plastic tubs

of candied salmon chunks. Timed circuits snap
off lights to save power. Some workers rise

to renew the glow; most pack up, head out
for drinks.
Driving home with necktie coiled

on the seat beside him, still unsure
what to do, Connor snorts at radio

reports of a knife-sporting crow, an aged judge
handcuffed in the park for being Black,

a yearling black bear arrested
at the opera;
he daydreams of oncoming

dump trucks jumping the divider, smashing
him lifeless, but *Killing yourself is quitting,*

he thinks, *what Dad did to Mom and me*. Home,
he logs into his console to shut down

his mind, clears labyrinths of CG ghouls
to calm down before his date. It works –

making his player character juke
lumbering undead and explode their groaning heads

restores Connor's sense of normality
till his in-game avatar gets snagged

in the glitchy seam between two polygons
of a rendered wall – not dead, not playing

but flickering in place, forced to choose
between rebooting or waiting for a loose

ghoul to finish him off. In frustration, he unplugs
the games machine, the big-screen TV –

feels the fear of capture wake again
as the loft quiets.
Downstairs, trading pressures,

bodily densities, and scents, a pair of lovers
perfects their collaboration. *For this afterglow,*

the couple laughs, *we'd do it even if it hurt.*
Across the lane, a violinist jerks his bow

across the strings, stroking from his instrument
inimitable licks of bliss. The tones

of a rich tenor voice rise and fade away
as a squat Calabrian man strides by

cantillating *O Sole Mio* like a sacred text.
Strangers lean from open windows to stare

and call *Bravo. What's rehearsal?* Connor wonders
*and what's performance?*
Coral leaves Adanac HQ

as thrushes whistle on the chicken wire.
She snakes between muddy potholes

to the road's shoulder, hikes north to a bus stop
beyond the reservation. Swimming slowly

against the traffic flow, her bus arrives late
to the bar Mark named. She's pleased with it –

the kind of taproom she doesn't mind,
with seating outside, a brick-paved terrace

with cast-iron tables and chairs. Inside,
she finds Mark relating some anecdote

that has the braces-wearing bartender
in stitches. Over the bar's hum she can't

hear what her husband's saying but sees
he's happy – Mark spots her and smiles wider,

eyes dime-like with excitement. Her milder
smile dims to a grimace when he slaps

not the corporate card, but cash on the bar,
He steers her to where their employees sit,

saying: *Don't worry, Coral! You worry*
*too much! You guys,* he says to their workers,

*covered a hell of a lot of ground today.*
*Find anything fun on your travels?*

*Old jackknife,* says Sandy, *in the framing.*
*You keep it?*
                                        *Nah. Sealed it up again.*

*No porn?* asks Mark, and the table groans.
*I'm bored of finding porn,* says Jamie, *Why can't people*

*hide anything else?*
                                                    *What else have they got to hide?*
asks Hardeep.
                                        Coral answers: *What they truly*

*stand for*, and licks salt crystals from
her celery stalk. Coral smiles to cheer

the guys, moves her olive arms
smoothly to pin up her coils

of coffee-coloured hair, to lay
her phone on the table face-down.

*At least you won,* she says to Mark. He frowns.
*Of course I did. I play to win.*
*You said you'd stop.*

He gives her a look that says: *Not here, not now.*
*Nice place,* she says. *Good pick,* and leaves

for the ladies' room while he cools off.
Mark samples Coral's Caesar, and

Viró

props her borrowed six-speed on a bollard,
takes stock of phablets and phones that drinkers

have left trustfully on tables. Her stomach constricts
as it always does when she's forced to this.

She reiterates: *You're doing this for art,*
*to save the sacred thing you made. They'll all*

*buy new phones. For them, just one more bleep on the*
*credit card,*
*but everything to you. Now, one, now*

*two, now move on through,* and she saunters cooly
through the patio, bussing smeared glassware

as if she worked there, bagging unwatched windfalls
in cases of black rubber, pastel silicon,

and mother of pearl with printed roses.
Shaking like a drop on a goblet's lip,

Viró hops back on the borrowed bike, pedals
out of sight before she dismounts, disables

the phones' self-trackers with trembling hands,
dropping screws in her haste. Half her mind

is home the whole time – boiling pasta,
dusting Kraft parma on pre-made

sauce, singing along to *Casiotone*
*for the Painfully Alone* songs on YouTube.

Her other half's intent on the task, on
closing the gap between "have" and "need"

before that gulf fills up with loss, or shame,
or fear of eternal flame.
*Two more bars,*

*then home. Then rest.*
A voice inside her asks:
*Then what? Tomorrow – twice as much? Five days*

*just aren't enough.*
*But what choice do I have*
*except to try? Should I take whatever deal*

*that shark will make?*
She remounts, buzzes downhill
into the evening wind.
Mark's beard twitches

when Coral gets back, asks about her phone.
*Here, I left it here. In a pearly case,*

*with roses.*
Mark's eyebrows rise.
*Oh Lordy! Mark,*
*it's just plastic. Where is it?*
*Maybe*, says Mark,

*you dropped it. Why're you always losing things?*
The guys chuckle, caught between pretending

Mark's joking, and pretending not to hear.
Coral churns her celery stalk around her drink, sees

satisfaction spread across her husband's face
as he puts all the blame on her.
Wind whipping

her wintry hair, Viró passes the offices
her father once patrolled. Here he monitored

a lattice of CCTVs, strolled halls
with brazen keys tinkling at his belt

before his arteries eclipsed. Viró recalls
how her boiler-bellied father

who liked to smoke shirtless in a snowstorm
then shivered whatever he wore, crept from chair

to chair forever out of breath, and died
while pulling on his shoes, leaving no worldly

legacy but estranged siblings in the arctic,
his daughter, petty debts, and somewhere

an ex-wife who'd only darken his door
to beg, wiggling polka-dotted acrylic nails

at Viró peeking from the hallway closet.
Viró wonders where her mother is now; why she

never came in, said *Bye-bye, Johnniebo*
so fast and never looked back – even that time

Viró came out, stood in plain sight to watch
her mother get in a rusty truck and

cough at a strange man to drive.
In office-blocks,
a remnant of workers let windows

light their desks, the sun's radiant field expanding
palpably through the air, painful on surfaces.

Having worked without break since morning, Feng
listens for cathedral bells to bless

her labours' end. But no bells sound
as six o'clock goes by; the change-ringer

must be late today, or sick. Feng's claim-proofing
the puffery of a junior miner's prospectus,

trying to lend an air of dignity to –
*What was it Kipling called a mine? A hole*

*owned by a liar. And what's a hole that men*
*like Murray flog with orangutang-like hands,*

*subs run through pseudonyms, sidelines in crypto?*
*Maybe it's all straight. Maybe they're salting samples,*

*it's a pump n' dump.*
*Clients don't need to be saints,*
Feng reminds herself, *they just have to pay.*

Sunlight hits her left hand where it clicks
the keyboard, threatens to scald the skin

time has started to thin. She doesn't know
why she works through lunch for crooks,

books profits she can't spend since anyhow
Meghan will be cared for by the Crown

when Feng's dead, and nothing Feng can do
will hurt or help or alter that...
*except*

*to rent, maybe, a brighter, more scenic*
*sanatorium for my daughter to wreck.*

Unwelcome, unwelcome thoughts.
At last
the chimes sound from Corpus Christi's belfry:

Do *Mi* Re *Sol*; Do *Re* Mi *Do*
Mi *Do* Re *Sol*; Sol *Re* Mi *Do*.

When Feng hears *Messiah* at Christmas,
the bells' tune sounds behind the line

*I know that my redeemer liveth*. And the words
Feng hears are sung by her daughter's

Brownies group, long ago – at meeting's close
they stood to pray – little girls in *café au lait*

uniforms and badged chocolate sashes
like a battery of candy bells sang

*O Lord this week, Thy Children seek.*
*Good deeds to do, And to be true.*

The chime fades. Six bare notes mark
the end, *A-men A-men A-men,*

but Feng thinks of Meghan, three decades on,
stuck: *Is that word right – stuck – or is she adrift?*

Reflexively trying to pinpoint where
she erred, Feng assembles a mental timeline

of Meghan's benders after grad, her first break
and treatment, her anger after the shards

knocked back together but never quite reknit.
Feng deep down believes some harshness on her part,

some omitted care allowed the fraying to start,
let the illness enter her daughter's brain.

*Heal my child,* Feng prays each night, *God, heal*
*my precious child.*
                                        Feng dislikes the ploys

Meghan's illness adopts, how it doses her
with weed, E, ayahuasca, makes Meghan

eat only pizza and ice-cream, drowse
on a hide-a-bed all day. *What is a sickness*

*that works through the will? What's it all for,*
*if I can't help my girl?*
                                             Feng hums to herself

the Brownie hymn:
          *O Lord our God; Thy Children call.*
          *Grant us Thy Peace and Bless us all.*
                                                                   *What blessing?*

Feng's heart asks, moving her sinewy hand
from the scalding light. *What's it all for?*

Unwelcome thoughts – she wants to stop. Feng packs
for home: stubs in earbuds, taps

the triangle. Woodwinds lisp; violins sob,
blotting out tears she wills herself to control.

## DINNER

Holding back their cheers, Wildlife Control
watches the sedated bear rouse in a sub-alpine

meadow. Ravens cluck in disappointed
pines, plumes interlocked like snake-scales down their backs.

Still a little stoned, the freed bear looks around,
amazed to wake in the mountains – seeming

to have dreamed the clock's concrete maze,
the sour-smelling cave where his nightmare

faded to a green less lit than blackness.
Plagued with a headache, he sucks fuzzy blooms

from shrubs, stumbling north down a disused FSR.
Wildlife Control high-five and hug – unfed

ravens glide elsewhere. Along the shoreline,
slate-blue herons alight on rocks and docks

where ocean water laps, wafts crabs and shiners
past to attract the heron's sudden stab.

Mid-ocean, the tireless swells roll shoreward.
Clouds brew in the troposphere where Jack

overflows his window seat. A tray
of salmon and rice arrives, a plastic

ramekin of creme brûlée, a glass
of chilled rosé. He puts away the laptop

with which he's been reading up on unsolved
risks with transplants, flips the napkin

across his lap and checks his Patek Philippe,
already set to Bangkok. Jack knows by now

bullion is being packed for him
in HSBC's vault - a metric tonne

of gold in small but heavy crates.
He looks out
through acrylic panes, past the pinhole's frost flecks

onto expansive plains of clouds, still bright in the sun
he's chasing west. Jack knows he won't sleep

on the long flight. The sun has slowed
its descent for him while his O-Con profits

remain in physical gold, so small they could
almost be swallowed by a fish. He's never

felt vulnerable like this, his wealth's never felt
so ephemeral, but he couldn't take the chance

marooned Connor would take revenge
by spurring police (normally lethargic)

into freezing Jack's accounts before he lands.
He's more reliant on Kittisak, his Thai agent

than he would have liked, Jack thinks,
chewing a mouthful of sockeye, but *Loyalty*,

as Jack tells anyone that listens, *is one*
*part inspiration, nine parts perspiration.*

He's grateful to have Kittisak around –
a man he's made sweat since boyhood,

who's in awe of Jack as you revere
a man who's given you all you have

and fear him too, since he can retract
the gifts. *One part inspiration,*

*nine parts perspiration,* Jack mentally repeats
with pride. *Never a bhat astray*

*with Kitty in twenty years, never a button*
*out of place.* He pictures the smile on Kitty's face

whenever he meets Jack in arrivals, rolls
Jack's luggage out to their pink Evoque.

*I'll need a new car,* he thinks, *now I'm a new man.*
No more Evoque, with its rakish flair.

He'll trade it in for something more demure –
a Merc, perhaps, or a vintage Phantom.

He sips his rosé, looking out the window
at waveless fields of cloud, at the bent

limit of the world.
Meghan bravely wears
smears of dried tears on her cheeks, browsing wares

on skid-row sidewalks: a blend of mongo
with the fruits of petty theft. In the park

where she picked salmonberries, the healer
had confirmed the worst – but now she feels the buzz

of apostles who teach a gospel of rebirth
behind locked doors lest the gentiles hear

and take it for their own.
*One size fits all*,
the hawker boasts, as Meghan selects a coat

with bangled drawstrings at hips and waist
and bust.
She almost yearns to be blatant

with curves, but feels protective of her secret
as she shops for something to disguise

the ways her shape will change as the sacred thing
she bears within her grows.
Diners' eyes

rove over Le Croc's hostesses in slick
black dresses, wine racks agleam

with glossy bottles, ivory napkins
with green, gold, and crimson nile crocodiles

embroidered round the rim. Elated,
gesturing with her glass, Vanessa babbles

to Connor about her forthcoming play,
relating what the audience will like,

what scenes need work, her itch for fold-out
effects designed by Viró, and *en passant*

relates the tale of Viró scrambling to save
her creation, before sketching out casting calls,

fundraising efforts, rehearsal schedules, and
finally rising from the table to mime

out plans for blocking.
Connor's annoyed,
but can tell she's really talking to herself,

saying all this aloud so she doesn't lose
the non-stop thoughts bubbling up from some spring

inside her. When Vanessa's talk runs dry,
*Better advertise,* he teases, *make box office*

*so you can afford to stop wearing knock-offs,*
*embarrassing me like this.*
Vanessa frowns, though

this is well-trodden ground. *It's good value,*
she says. *No one can tell.*
*Everyone can tell.*

*You're one to talk*, she smirks with burning cheeks,
*wearing black basketball shoes with chino slacks.*

He peeks under the table, sees his jet
Airs opposite her lilac Vans.

*From the ankle down,* he grants, *we match,*
*and from the neck up…*
Connor pinches

the Tiffany box in his pocket, thinks
of saying *We could match our hands and lives,*

and popping the lid, proposing right there,
but then thinks *What for? O-Con's*

*a ticking bomb, and I'm the only one around*
*to answer for the wreckage when it blows.*

Vanessa sees his hand drop to his pocket,
his intent turn inward. She's flattered,

but when their eyes meet, Connor spies
inside her pupils his own twinned likenesses

in paired aquaria. Connor's face
goes blank, his hands grip cutlery. He stoops

to his dish, forks sous-vide deer meat to his lips,
lapsed into daydreams
                                        of tackling

a rogue shooter who'd erupt from
a nearby table – knocking the gun

aside too late to save himself… bullets
thud through his chest before he snaps

the shooter's neck between his hands, sinks
with his rival to the floor, rust-smelling gouts

pushed from wounds where bullets ran in and out.
He imagines Vanessa cradling his form

like something precious, an adoring mob
reverencing, grateful, glad, as he lifts

his sticky scarlet hands like a priest
to bless them all, anoint Vanessa's forehead

with a smudge of blood.
                                        At first, Vanessa
pouts; then feels baffled by how he sweats

when talk resumes, the way his tongue flicks
at the corner of his lips when she asks

about his day. Nervous? She's still unsure
how to answer if he does propose, knows

she can retract a "yes" but not a "no."
She tracks his enervated gaze over tables

of high school grads dining on their way to proms,
romantic pairs, and reuniting friends.

Reaching for an olive branch, she says
*I saw something after work today.*

*Walking along the beach. An old guy*
*and little kid pulled a dead seal*

*from the waves. Stroked it with bare hands before*
*they towed it out to sea and let it go.*

*Uncanny. Like a sequence from a myth,*
*it felt staged without the staging.*

*There was a hole – like a bullet hole – in the seal,*
*still bleeding. Why would anyone shoot a seal?*

*Maybe it shot itself*, jokes Connor. Vanessa scoffs,
but wishes she hadn't when Connor adds

*like dad did, right through the heart.*
Vanessa
shakes her head prettily, not sure if it's true

or a trick to wrongfoot her. *He was broke.*
*Debts right and left. My mom made me swear*

*not to be like him.*
She says he's not.
Connor chews. Swallows twice.
*You think*

*my dad took the cowards' off-ramp?*
*No, I...*
*the ones who... that, it's their only way out?*

*No better choice?*
*Guess not.*
She tastes her meal:
acidity and sweetness, the meat's umami

flavours saturate her senses, until she
sees Connor wiping his plate with sourdough,

mopping up smears of myoglobin mixed
with gastrique, somber as a priest dabbing

drips from a dying communicant's lips.
She's far from finished, but Connor flags down

the sommelier, orders dessert as if
Vanessa weren't there. Fair play, she supposes,

if rude – she never orders her own sweet
when asked. She resigns her food: aligns

her knife and fork at five o'clock, handles
oiled with fingerprint whorls. Waiters reset

the table, grant a discreet pause before
Connor's panna cotta comes, polka-dotted

with sour purées of cherry and nectarine,
dark vanilla flecks nesting in cool cream.

Connor's spoon dips and lifts to his tongue:
the malic fizz of esters, unctuous splash

of milk fat in a mouthful of enzymes
fail to free him from memories of

his father's aftermath:
courtrooms bleak
as the bottom of the sea, abrading

his father's estate to sand;
his mother
ambling naked down the highway, sad flesh

lit up by headlights that slowed to watch.
Vanessa accepts the second spoon,

and when the panna cotta's gone, Connor
calls for the bill and a fresh coffee-press,

knowing Vanessa's shifts at the café
leave her sickened by the smell.
                                        With bitter,

sweet, tart, and sour to taste, what craving
drives us to troll, tease, infuriate friends

or strangers in online markets of likes and links?
Does it do more than scratch our itch

to think we've glimpsed a secret,
grant us the relief of lapsing into automatic

thoughts, talking on autopilot like bots
that phish with lures of greed and fear:

> *YOU ARE INFECTED / NASTASYA (19)*
> *WANTS TO CHAT / CLICK HERE TO CLAIM YOUR PRIZE*

though the kingdom of the clock absolves us
from being known, offers us the thrill

of knowing we could shove a stranger
onto subway tracks and run free, unrecognized

by crowds whose testimony won't agree
on height, or race, or shape of face.
                                        Anna

resists the urge to refresh her email
while a veterinary tech with tennis

player's figure and Mitteleuropean
accent feels Percy's feet for breaks. Samson

peruses comments on his posts about the bear,
his free hand idly stroking Percy's ears.

Wanting to think he witnessed an act
of kindness, Samson's shocked by trolls

who say the yearling was euthanized,
its furry body left for ravens at the dump.

*What's it all for,* he wants to know, *if death*
*is what they want?*
Anna asks *Did it break?*

Percival yips, the vet tech injecting
his paw with painkiller.
*Yes. I'll put*

*a boot on it, but he'll need Percocet*
*until the bone and tendons knit.*
Anna feels

relieved, though the fracture's no better
than she feared. For penitence, she'll pay

the vet's ludicrous bill, dose the dog's meals,
and won't wear heels at home again.
*Crown Royal*

*in its purple plush's a treat like the President*
*drinks,* Glen gloats as he enlarges his ego

by imbibing one bottle. His boasting
becomes a rant against his brother Ken:

*High and mighty for a fairy who lives*
*underwater,* he tells the seagulls, who

cock their heads skeptically
as he explains *Not that I judge! Love's love!*

He knows it's unwise, but flushed with his own
magnificence, loosens the second drawstring,

cracks a second plastic cap. This time,
the whisky shrinks him to an ant's size,

tunes his antenna to the snakes' frequency
until not only *l'appel du vide*

is hissing in his ears but *l'appel du mal*
as well. Soon he's back on the rooftop parking lot

where he likes to watch for dawn,
taking a pee onto tourists posing

for photos, gleefully slinging gravel
at pairs promenading below. By the time

cops come stomping up the stairs, Glen's unable
to rise, sprawled in an empty stall. He spits

in the first cop's face, who wipes the gob away
with hate. Ashamed of himself, and appalled

by his whisky paralysis, Glen atones
by hocking a mouthful of mashy froth

on himself. *Why this disgrace?* he asks himself,
*Why abase myself like this?* With less gentleness

than past arrests, familiar cops who call him
*Glenner*, and *Fuckface*, cuff him, stuff him

in the drunk tank where he won't lie still,
and clangs on the untuned bars of the cell

to be let free.
In his sailboat's galley,
Samson's father preps ramen on his Primus.

Enoch's had a day of it with his boy.
They shared the tanker; the bear's capture

and seal's funeral; shared leaves and stones
and wires, congelations of city light.

Now Enoch's tired, his mind niggles at how
Anna's bullet-like self only shows

when she's in motion, how he can only paint
what's in repose. Grown old with the night shift

still to work, he snips the foil cachet of stock.
His knuckles ache. In his frayed breast pocket,

a cellphone speaker tinnily replays
baroque laments that ease his pain. Enoch

loves and is lonely inside his brittle jar
of bones, but he knows how Samson lit up

when they met in the schoolyard,
and smiled coming home on the pilot's boat

with his childish hair blown back. Under the pot,
propane flames sway like windblown hair or grass

in tune with the choir and accompanying tremolos
of reeds and strings. A home on the waves

is a rocking hammock, a womb. Nylon rope
ties prow to buoy and stainless steel links

chain to the ocean floor where sand dabs
flutter in silt – blind sinistral side down,

double-eyed dexter up. What do these
twisted fish see with uncomplicated eyes?

Blued light. Vague shadows turning, or seeming
to turn. Flickering thin fins of sky.

## NIGHTFALL

Cigarettes flick from fingers. The sky glows
brighter than dark shores where herons pose, outlined

necks bent back like bows. Feasting gulls
wheel like a winged crown above a dead seal

floating out to sea. Every eye can tell
what time it is – shadows of trees and towers

stretch east in retreat, while the gnomons
they grow from turn on their flywheel of stone.

*Work hard, Play hard – but Play's more fun by far:*
a creed we quote at the bar, charging

the Firm's card for drinks. As the sun's eye
thins to a gold band, oft-divorced bosses

flirt with summer interns: promise plums
to the hot ones, present themselves as prime mentors,

play GoPro clips on phones. Swinging dicks gulp
cocktails while juniors sip, sensing

the recklessness of lonely men. Even more
than for sex, tonight there's an appetite

for fellowship as felt on atavistic ships
exploring fjords, when ancestors avoided

embassies of other forefathers who stood
saluting in their dugout canoes. No wonder

the citizens work late –
                                        no wonder they
crowd bleachers to cheer a Brazilian rookie

who chases the skipping ball, tames it,
dekes, leaps a defender's knee, leads himself

while converging with the keeper – both slide,
spritzing rubber beads from turf. The rookie's foot

gets first to the ball, shoots the sewn globe
of chrome pentagons past spread

fluorescent gloves, makes the nylon net go
*tching*. We roar for the new recruit's first goal,

*rah, rah* – until: *He's deaf,* someone shouts,
and *Deaf, that kid's born deaf* ripples through the crowd.

As the rookie leaps in his team's embrace,
fans start to stamp their feet – *right*, *left*, *right*, *left* –

till their champion looks up, startled at thrums of worship
transmitted through the ground. Then his eyes

swim so bright fans gasp and weep, hold up
their hands like holy rollers in the spirit,

fill the stadium with cheers.
Along footpaths
by the waterfront, walked dogs drop blobs of poo

while owners trade compliments and tips, yank
curious pups from the aromatic

trails of skunks. Couples watch raccoons sortie
from a hollow elm, a sore doe grazing

while twin fawns chase her teats from lawn to lawn.
*Should we give up the sea,* we endlessly

debate, *learn to live within our means?*
*Life's cheaper inland, rent's low – though you can't see*

*the sun's stretched reflections fill waves*
*with brazen fish, can't watch seals or seagulls*

*glide lazily through saltchuck and sky.*
*Should we give up the sea? Rather, we would give up*

*all the earth, live aboard a floating world*
*as we do in dreams.*
The sun's band snaps,

the sky goes dark. Stuck in traffic mid-
bridge, Vanessa can't help feeling down, humming

tunes like "Too Gone Too Long." Her phone pings; the screen
glows with an old friend's kudos. Connor's eye

is drawn to the black glass beyond her shoulder,
where his own dour double glowers above

her better-lit reflection thumbing a reply.
*Why'd I talk about my dad tonight?* He can't

decide what to do about O-Con: run
or play dumb, and shame's composting in his cells,

excreting heat and a humid vapour
only he can smell. He thinks of the sea below,

of the Haida "Spirit of Wealth" whose sea-floor
longhouse was robbed for matter used to make

the mortal world, and how the Romans named
their death god "Father of Wealth," whose house

also was found in unsounded depths. *If only*
*what they believed was true,* he thinks, *I could*

*dive down, dredge up the wealth I need. But all*
*there is, is atoms and the void.*
His palms

slither on the steering wheel, greased by the oils
they ooze. The ring box goads his thigh. Dying

to stop Vanessa's humming, Connor bops the horn –
his leased Mazda bleats. *What's wrong?* she asks.

*We've time.*
Connor imagines admitting
*O-Con's just a scam gone bad*,

but even in this fantasy it isn't himself
telling Vanessa the truth, but some puppet self

existing just for that confession.
In motors idling all around, Connor hears

something sibilant, snickering at
the descendants of shrews in fancy cars

pretending to matter. Part of Connor
is frightened, part welcomes its offer

of total freedom – *You owe them nothing,*
he thinks, and stomps the gas – his hatchback

bends fenders with the Porsche ahead.
Vanessa yelps at the impact as her long neck

whips. The rear-ended driver gets out:
a bigger, older man. Reminded of Jack,

Connor bounces from his seat and slaps
the old man's face. A shriek of outraged shock

adds to the warnings Connor's trying
to ignore. *What's it all for?* he wonders.

*Maybe all along, Dad had it right.* He hauls
himself up to stand on the bridge rail.

Holding steel cables in terrified hands
to keep steady in his high-tops, he looks past

the archipelago of ships, past facing shores
that separate north from south, to fiery clouds

in the far west, still basking in a sunset
he can't see. *The air's cleaner out here,*

he thinks, *no one knows where the frightened soul*
*goes when the only home it's known is broken.*

*Could be the House of Riches. Could be*
*another shot at life.*
He hears a hiss

from the blackness below, the hoarse curses
of the hurt man behind him, Vanessa's screams.

*Mom won't care*
*You owe them nothing* sizzles
in the air and he leans out – *Fuck you*, he calls

and lets his oily hands release. Suddenly
cold and clean, Connor exalts in the brief grace

of weightlessness before taut whispers
swell to a wordless roaring while he falls.

## LAMP-LIGHTING

Recordings of the day fade from recall
and self-accusations are shelved as Anna

eats ice cream on the couch with Samson.
Her son narrates his afternoon with Enoch –

steering a stranded tanker out to sea
while nestlings chimed under the bridge deck,

the dead seal in the waves, and falling bear
caught in a vaudeville net.
                    Anna's glad

he's safe, not sure about the rest. Often
she's blamed Enoch for painting in silence

with their son, for how Samson comes home
seeming slighted and unseen, but she's alarmed

by the opposite extreme, even if...
she pictures Enoch and Samson half-naked,

a scrawny pair on a beach where fitness buffs
play topless volleyball, and smiles. Samson asks

about the comments he saw online; she
weighs the matter, says the kingdom does

what's cheapest: it's cheaper to free a bear
in the hills than kill it. Samson tells her

his surprise at smelling its musk
from where they watched. Anna recounts

coasting with Enoch past exposed rocks
where bears grazed on the mussel beds – how wind

would carry the beasts' ripe scent to them,
clear as the crack of bivalves between teeth.

As if parodying the bears, Percy
snarfs cheese sticks on the floor, the boot

on his paw and plastic cone making percussive
scrapes and pings on the parquet. After dessert,

the duo watch TV, Samson in PJs,
Anna in slip. Anna's hating herself again

for hurting the dog, for lying in court, hating
the judge for hearing her lie.
*What's it all for?*

Anna wonders. She yearns for what she felt
on the train platform before work, but that feeling

seems to glitter from a distance, dwindling,
less easy to perceive as it recedes. Without warning,

Samson leans over, lays his hard, small head
in his mother's lap. He does not do this

often anymore. Wondering if this
is the last time, Anna lifts her left hand

to smooth the fluff of her son's soft hair.
So strange: she feels like a ghost, amazed

by a beauty beyond herself and like a child
powerless, pulsing with simple joy. Across

the clay-grey sky, crows retreat *en masse*
to industrial exurbs out east, where

they'll bulk out the boughs of silhouetted trees
like tar-black leaves and fill the gravel yards

of relic factories.
                    Viró's cold
and tired, biking home. Phones, both poached and purchased

clatter in her satchel when she stops, props
her foot on the curb at a lonely red light.

A police cruiser rolls up, halts. The cop
riding shotgun eyes Viró, knows despair

when she sees it, registers how Viró
hides in baggy clothes, wears blue hair

like a nom de guerre. Viró watches
the trained gaze puzzle over pink Band-Aids

on fingertips, flick to her wastrel face.
Viró fixes her stubborn stare on a far red spark

atop a tower till she feels the cop's eyes drop
away, unable to pinpoint what addiction lures

Viró through this labyrinth. *What's it all for?*
the artist asks herself. *To give physical form*

*to some ideas? Why not, like Nessy,*
*say yes to what they offer?*
                                        Viró pictures

the bliss Vanessa's chasing with Big –
a man's aging body to love, kids, dogs,

an island getaway, Christmases
at the ski chalet. What's not to like?

So why does Viró feel abhorrence, as if
her friend were setting out to mine for metals

toxic to the touch?
                                        She doesn't know, and
throws that copper thought into the gulf

between herself and normalcy.
                                                        Green light.
Police cruiser turns politely left. Viró

pedals home, ambivalent and alone.
                                                                Bridge
closed for a jumper, a lineup of static traffic

idles. Coral's had a few drinks, she's
making eyes at Mark, reclining

on their pickup's bench seat so her shirt
draws tight across her breasts, rubbing

her left foot on Mark's right thigh.
*So*, Mark laughs, *what do you want to do*

*when we get home?*
                                        *Oh… You know,* she says,
still buzzed from drinks and the day's success.

*Some things I like. Maybe some things you like too…*
She starts to sing *Get down tonight,*

shimmying on the seat.
                                        *You're drunk,*
Mark observes approvingly.
                                                    *Too drunk to drive,*

she hums, *Mmm hmm. But not too drunk*
*to ride.*
          Mark puts the truck in park,

unbuckles his seatbelt to lean across the cab
and kiss her quick, taste the fizz on her lips,

lick her eager tongue with his.
Her fingers hook his pockets, pull him down

before the car behind them honks, and he
sits up, retakes the wheel to close the gap

while her mournful hips relax. *How long till this goddam
jam clears up?*
Coral taps the stereo

on with her toe tip, turns it off. Flips
the A/C, on and off, assessing

the dexterity of her tipsy toes.
*Cut it out*, says Mark.
*Anything to read?*

she asks, looking behind the seat
for a magazine, pressing the glovebox

release, which doesn't give.
*Is this locked? Why?*
*Why darlin', my six-shooter's there,* Mark jokes.

*Cash?* Coral asks, *How much?*
He shrugs, rakes
fingers through his beard.
*Like hell you don't remember*,

she says, giving his ribs a kick. *You remember*
*who won the Stanley Cup in '68!*

*Habs*, he says, *that's easy, they won from*
*'65 to '69.*
*That's my point,*
*Mark, we weren't even born then. How much*

*cash was it today?*
Mark scratches his prickly beard,
trying to pinpoint the smallest amount

she'd believe.
*Lord in Heaven,* Coral moans,
*don't lie to me.*
*Not much,* he lies.
*Mark,*

*I love you, but listen. We can't afford*
*you gambling. We can't afford you hoarding*

*cash for the casino.*
*We were having such a nice night,*
Mark sighs. *Let's not wreck it now.*
Cars ahead

begin to move. When they reach home, both feel
beaten. Coral tries to borrow Mark's keys

to fetch the cash from his glovebox, but
*Leave it,* says Mark. *It's locked up safe. Come*

*love me.*
Amid the kingdom's stochastic litany,
its whine of sirens and groan of train wheels

a flash of flame gasps on the harbour wall
and a cannon's roar booms over baffled woods

where burnouts and the terminally lonely
slink from parked cars, find soft spots to die. Like stones

spat from the tarmac by spinning tires they vanish
into the wild world of story and understory,

where birds dismember carrion, squirrels
scrape skeletons for calcium.
At the nurse's desk,

Yusuf's a nuisance. He demands to know
why his wife's been abandoned, whether the admins

know their baby's high-risk with gastroschisis,
that Mary hasn't yet seen a doctor. *They said*

*a few minutes; we've been waiting an hour.*
*I'm not overreacting. We need our doctor*

*and birthing room, now. Please!* Yusuf rushes
back to Mary's side, trying not to let his fear

transform to fury. Mary breathes deep,
wishing Yusuf would get her mum on the phone,

but doesn't want to hurt his feelings
by asking. *We'll need a name,* she tells Yusuf

to soothe him. *What about Cyrus? Or Leo?*
Mary knows to keep herself on an even

keel, conserve her strength for the climax –
not yearn for the friends she's known since girlhood

who've also passed the test she's retaking –
not wish for those she misses to be whisked

across the sea. Through a smeared window, she
watches gulls pockmark the fragile sky; each

points toward the sandbanks where they'll sleep
on pink feet, ashy wings tucked back like cloaks,

unruffled by the breeze.
Home from his steakhouse,
Murray enters his housekeeper's suite. Inez

looks up, wide-eyed from the settee as if
surprised, but wearing the white-lace teddy

he gave her at Christmas. He holds his chin
high, sucks his potbelly in. Brave as an acrobat, Inez

catches his hairy frame as he collapses
on her chest. She helps him undress.

Her skin's hot on his – his flabby surfaces
feel chilled where they touch her limbs

but she doesn't flinch. *This is what I'm paid for,*
her kisses say, but *Poor, poor thing,*

say her caresses.
                    Once he's done, they detach,
and he's careful not to cling – careful not

to go beyond what she can stand, afraid
to tip his hand.
                    He knows he ought to sleep

but can't, even with the day's stains
freshly steam-cleaned from his bloodstream,

replaced with poppy-like perfumes. Racking
his brain for something to do, K303

comes to mind, the sculpture
his son had said to see.
                    *Why not tonight?*

He leaves his suit, white shirt, and power tie
for Inez to sort, pulls on a sweater, jeans,

nicks a mickey from the cupboard
to bring along. Lacing up his Nikes,

he tells Inez, *I've tried every kind of rye,*
*and the best rye whisky of all is still*

*the bargain kind you buy in plastic fifths*
*from hampers by the checkout till.*
Pain's

germinating again in Murray's veins
as if its spores lived latent in his soil –

he looks forward to loathing whatever he finds
in K303, to teasing his son

for lacking soul and letting his taste be tricked
by trash. He goes outside: on gravel rooftops,

ferns and saplings fuzz skyscraper summits
with downy life – bright islands in the night.

## BEDTIME

Block after block down aisles of night, Mehrdad
balances an umbrella in his left hand

against the granddaughter riding on his right.
Mary's list warned him that after stories, hot milk,

puppet-play, a half-hour of muted TV,
Larissa's bedtime would require this tour,

require them to recite "Goodnight!" to all they see.
*Goodnight, flower trees,* Larissa says. *Goodnight, flowers.*

*Goodnight, Grandpa Bozo's Buick. Goodnight raccoon.*
Cupped to one shoulder, the toddler looks up

inside the umbrella, delighting in an ambience
stained blue by the taut cloth, the tip-pat of raindrops

drumming down. *Goodnight, rain. Goodnight street.*
Water beads on the umbrella's ribs, glints

in letting go. *Goodnight ocean, trees, and towers,*
Mehrdad whispers as Larissa slumps, accepting

sleep: *Goodnight ships that sail the sea. Goodnight*
*to all the stars that we can't see.*
Mehrdad

turns back. Both hands full, he can't tip back up
the wool cap that keeps slipping over his eyes,

blinkering him with its brim in his hour
of triumph. Back aching, he wishes his wife

were there to witness the curly head at last
asleep, thinks of texting Yusuf, but cringes,

knowing Mary's pushing her sad burden
through the dark with Yusuf beside her.

Having lived grief to its limit, he knows
they'll endure, but not unscathed

if the baby's skin like Armin's crinkles back
onto its bones, goes darker and florid

with unfiltered toxins, while doctors trained
to emulate empathy act as if all

might still be well. *How frightened we are tonight!*
he thinks, while his eyes roam unfocussed

over honeycombs of rooms.
                                        Eastward past blocks
of power poles studded with old staples,

past tear-downs leased to students and artists
praying for different kinds of love,

past front yards full of dandelion clocks
and leaky roofs tented over with tarps,

a patrol car ferries Vanessa home. Like all cops,
these two know talking only makes it worse and let

Vanessa watch through Kohl-brushed lashes
the thinning out of raindrops under streetlights,

think over the call she made to Connor's mother,
who kept interrupting her condolences

to repeat with growing emphasis
*Even the maya is maya.*
                                        What was that

phrase supposed to express? She'd thought
of the formula again on the station steps,

pausing to toss two bucks to a long-lashed
man lolled flat, his blood-red Bulls vest soiled

as if from rolling in the dirt.
                                        Down aisles of night
the patrol car drives, parking at the Manor

where Vanessa rooms. There's a tune
in the night air – subtle, eternal – as Vanessa

traipses around the side of the house,
through uncut grass that soaks her lilac Vans.

On backyard clotheslines, paper lanterns
glow candy-colours – bearded boys

with rolled-up sleeves wear bow ties, women
sport flowery skirts from which tattoos

of ice-cream cones and radishes playfully peep.
Vanessa's friends and friends of friends sip drinks

from dollar-store goblets of candy-colour glass
while Debussy's themes pipe from the kitchen

and on the porch landing, a girl in a petticoat
and a smile two sizes too big begins to sing

"Le Tombeau des Naïades." Her trained voice
alloys with the tinny tinkling from inside,

holds the hushed assembly rapt. *What's it all for,*
Vanessa thinks, *if not to let us fail,*

*fuck up, and try again?* Her mascara finally streaks
with tears, but at the same time she attends to music

that hurts her like a headache, a tune she knew
but didn't know she knew.
                                        Citizens brush teeth,

toss in separate beds. Too sober to go home,
too footsore to walk on, Murray sits

on a stretch of drainage rock between
apartment blocks. He takes off shoes and socks,

kneads his knotted feet like gristly steaks.
Making no noise except the occasional clicks

of rocks he kicks, the flop of a sodden
face-mask he flicks aside, he eavesdrops on

a breakup's final scene unfolding
by the curb: a woman loads her car,

while her ex asks *why*, *why, why,* she explains
in tones too faint to hear – probably

*…it's not you it's me*, guesses Murray,
rehearsed so long it's wearisome to say.

Her ex tries to extract something he can
blame her for. But her trunk slams shut. The boy

implores her now, in a softer voice, to stay.
Her engine starts. She begs his pardon

and pulls away. Murray drains his mickey,
flips the plastic flask aside
                                        and climbs

to the park where field floodlights are still on
though the games are long over, and teams

long gone. Clouds orbit the copses, white
with the reflected gleam of LEDs. Moths flit

between the trees's leaves, filling the ill-lit
space with a flicker of wings while under

their shadows young couples cling closer,
excited by pheromones and fear of exposure.

Murray sneaks through the dark – half tipsy, half lost,
watchful and shy as an envious ghost.

Unseen pairs whisper and gasp
and Murray can picture their mouths agape,

the arching backs – how palms rub chests
and fingers pull – how denim rubs lycra,

acrylic strokes wool. With metallic sounds
as if their pinions dinged the moon's tin disc,

urban nighthawks dive, naming aloud the women
Murray's loved and excised from his life:

half pleased, half perturbed, he hears his exes
indexed: from Alma in the sixth grade

to Zora in his sixties – Laura,
Leticia, Ling-Ling, Maddy, Marge...
diverse

vox splice their melismas between the nighthawks
and regal tick-tocks of a million clocks:

dogs bay in backyards – freighters groan
as they float in and out of docks – hookups

hold their breaths in bathroom stalls of bars while
hand-dryers hum. Amid the noises, sleepless youths

and the sleepless old alike wash worries away
with vodka and pot, music's anodyne,

what's hot on YouTube, whatever helps
in blind depths where the dogfish hunt.

# OWL HOUR

In blind depths the dogfish grub
for flesh, and anyone who's been there knows

the benthos isn't where life begins
but where it goes. Currents spin the corpse

of Connor as it sinks, angling dead corneas
to mirror red and yellow sparks of living

light-strings. The chandelier siphonophores
that shine these lights aren't animals themselves

but aggregates of zooids too specialized
to live alone: one thing glows, another

sees; one's a stinger or stomach, one's a fin
or feeler. There's no meaning down here,

just calories, reproduction, rot. Fabric
woven from cotton and cashmere becomes

a frail shield against spiny sharks that skim
the blacked-out bottom. Dragged westward

by the ebb tide, Connor's stiff fingers
scrape the muddy floor of the abyss,

rouse clouds of silt until an armpit
hooks an anchor chain. Unable to drift

with the tide further without rising, inch by inch
up the chain's incline the body lifts

towards the still surface where a sailboat's buoy
bobs.
        TVs prattle to please exhausted

parents while toddlers sleep. Mehrdad pours
another pastis, streaming the *Baywatch* remake

while his first drinks settle in. Getting tipsy
on Pernod brought back from the shopping trip

where he lost, or almost lost, Larissa
reminds him again of his old disgrace –

the incident after the Shah's fall, when
his family wealth had vanished like a flock

of doves when a bus goes by. He'd been drunk,
morbidly reviewing their accounts' dregs,

when he noticed how Armin, far from stopping
their usual donations, had doubled them.

He started shouting, and when she yelled back
about "less fortunates" he grabbed her long neck

and shook her the way a dog shakes a gosling
in a slowed down moment, in which he felt panic

superimpose upon, and then efface his rage
as he read in Armin's face her agony

at seeing what he could be. He let go
her bruised throat and she raced to lock herself

in their bedroom – phoned 911 while he
begged for mercy through the hollow door.

After officers handed him a summons and left,
he emptied his Armagnac collection

into the bath and swore never to drink again
unless she poured it for him. She came to court

though he said she needn't – holding his arm
up the steps as if she'd trip without his help,

but regal in her Grace Kelly scarf,
tailored suit, amber quills impaling her jet-black bun.

She made him relax, while his legal-aid lawyer
and the prosecutor conferred in the hallway.

*You've got one witness, and she won't talk,*
his lawyer said. *I won't!* Armin protested,

when the prosecutor turned to size up
the guilty pair. By 11 o'clock a consent stay

was entered, and Mehrdad and Armin
walked out free to enjoy a holiday

while Yusuf was still in school. They explored
the art museum, discussed Cézanne and Monet.

Shy hands reached out to stroke each other's
sleeves as if to verify they were both

still there. Coming home for lunch, they instead
made love like newlyweds; afterwards, spent,

grateful Mehrdad admired her lines,
the artistry of her nude. To him she looked unchanged

since college, though Mehrdad's beard came grey
when he grew it. It was a comfort to him

to think he'd die before her. *I didn't,* he began,
but she cut him off with *I know you didn't*

and a kiss. *I mean*, he said, *I didn't*
*know I was capable of what I did.*

She smiled. *You'll be more careful now?*
*I will.*
*Then I'm not very sorry I called the police.*

*I'll feel bad about this my whole life long,*
he said.
          She asked *Do you want to make*

*another baby?* her voice sounding suddenly
unsure.
          A pair of miscarriages proved

their clock had run out, but still
it was a time of love. Now he drinks to kill

the days, to fall asleep the faster. *But who*
*can sleep tonight?* he thinks. *Mary is lifting*

*a black trap from the depths not knowing if*
*it holds a child or corpse. Yet this night, too,*

he realizes, *is a time of love.*
*Goftare nik, pendare nik, kerdare nik,*

he recites after a pause, energized by thoughts
of how *Armin would be praying now,*

*not picturing the worst.* He clicks off the TV,
racks his cloudy brains for sacred words.

*May evil perish.* His father taught him prayers
to say on waking and at night; Armin

shared the same lines with their children before bed,
while he read Bamdad's verse, smoked cigarillos

on the deck. Phrases long memorized revive,
take form. His eyes fixate on the reflected gaze

staring back at him from the TV's blackened screen,
and Mehrdad recites a garbled Pata-no:

> *O All-wise Lord and Holy Spirit,*
> *do not destroy the living creation of Asha.*

*May evil perish. May death end.*
*May decay wither in the North.*

*May evil and its creations perish,*
*and never threaten the living again.*

He pours his pastis down the drain, fetches
milk and tips it in a cup. Good thoughts,

good words, good deeds – but feels confounded,
outfoxed by outliving his wife:
                                        *What has*

*Larissa learnt, without Armin to teach her?*
*What will the grandson think about the world*

*if he survives?*
                        Feng lies in bed, watching
lights from passing cars slice across her room

in time to the hiss of tires. Feng's used to
her daughter making noise downstairs all night,

but Meghan hasn't stayed out so late
since her last spell of psychosis
                                        *– Crash –*

something's struck her window's trembling glass.
Feng sits up startled, sees an owl sway, dazed

on the wide windowsill, shakily turn
and glide away. Feng comes to the window

to look at the shape it left like a painting
on the pane. No cracks, just lines and smudges

of waxy dust – the owl's winged form
impressed as if in snow. Her eyes refocus

on the sidewalk below, spot movement
through gaps in the laurel hedge. Humming

*I know that my daughter liveth*, Feng waves
at Meghan shuffling up their walkway. Three

pairs of drawstrings swing from Meghan's coat,
plastic baubles on their ends refracting

the ambient light.
*What kind of coat is that?*
The image clicks. She's seen that design before:

winter wear in a maternity store.
*Wearing it by mistake? Or is there*

*no mistake?* Feng's heart leaps with longing
after a hope she long ago let go. Hope strains

against its limits, and Feng reviews
the men she's seen leaving Meghan's door:

*There's at least some chance the father's Chinese*,
Feng concludes, *if there is a child*. Her heart buzzes

like a wasp against a mirror, seeing
a wider life beyond, not knowing

if it's real. She feels her future teeter
on an edge, and aches to know which angle

she'll fall down.
Coral's hand gropes
into the empty dip in the mattress

where Mark should be. A rustle. She sits up.
It's Mark buttoning his black and white shirt,

clinching the Jack O' Diamonds belt buckle
he only wears for cards.
                                        *Where you going?*

she asks, still drowsy, nocturnal braid flopped
between her breasts.
                                        She hears a rustle: Mark's lips

moving in the sun-dried brambles of his beard.
*Please don't,* she begs. *What's it all for, if you lose*

*what we make?*
                                        *You need a new phone,* he says.
Coral doesn't take the bait. *We need,* she says,

*to stop the bleeding.*
                                        *But I'm about to get hot, baby,*
*really hot,* Mark blurts out, and Coral

can't help herself either, begins to cry. Mark
scratches his beard with a grimace as he

shoulders through the door. Dressed as the man
he longs to be, Mark drives at highway speed

towards the casino's purple lights, their radiation
mirrored on the river.
                                        Coral throws on

her kimono, beelines for the secret
pack of smokes taped in a Ziploc

to the back of the sink. Lying awake
with her black-haired sisters while their mother

paced from yard to porch in a haze of smoke,
she'd sworn it wouldn't happen to her. Now

she thinks of her father's life after he quit –
his knack for telling tales to delight the table,

how he romped with her sisters' kids in snow
and at the memorial, how GA mentees

spoke of the goodness he lived to show.
*Something's broken in Mark's brain,* thinks Coral,

*that I can't fix. All I can do is wait.*
Murray
limps through the foyer at the disused factory

he's been refitting as apartments
bit by bit, knowing it'll be cheaper to pay fines

legalizing units where tenants already live
than apply for permits ahead of time.

K303's been a pest since she moved in:
paying late, quoting the *RTA*. He'd have

evicted her sooner if the unit
was legit, but until zoning's fixed, tenants

are worth being patient with. He knocks. The dark
under the door tells him her lights are off,

she's likely out. He lets himself in:
sees light leak from the tiny bathroom, hears

the shower hiss.
It's a sad room. His shoe soles
scrape the unfinished concrete floor. He flicks

the lights on, prepared to tell the tenant
she can fuck off and die if she objects

to the visit. He scans the room for what Paul
thought he'd want to see. Wax models? A mess?

He looks up.
It takes him a few moments
to process what he's seeing, as birds

who've hit a sheet of glass take a string
of heartbeats to know what's happened. He stoops,

lies on his back as whiffs of white dust lift
from the floor.
*What are these winged figures? Gods?*

*Or the inner spirits of natural things?*
*Are those droplets shed by the man or tree*

*or snakes and rats the spirit's blades have sliced?*
*What do the cupbearers want the droplets for?*

He feels sick.
*Sad spirits, circling above.*
He doesn't know why he feels this way.

*It's late.*
There's a lid he doesn't often
crack, but now it's off and thrown aside.

The bottomless black lake beneath stares back.
Chill air breathes on the water's single eye.

*An economy of pain? Of grace?*
Murray returns to the mortal world

on the unfinished floor. His worn-out throat
is shaking but he brushes back

unwelcome thoughts like a swarm of bugs,
heaves back onto his knees, probes his pocket

for the mickey of rye he already
drank dry and threw away. He feels moved

to pour out an offering, an opposing
impulse to drink himself blind.
                                        He hears

the shower's hiss stop, drip and drop. Murray
breathes two deep lungfuls, moves to flick off

the light-switch, and leaves undetected,
tender as a half-healed cut. An automated

part of him, the Collector, recognizes
the Cape Dorset influence on forms that merge

animal and soul with implements, and knows
he needs this sculpture for his own – should toss

the tenant at dawn. The butcher's son is wary
of what will happen if he does.
                                        From vents

on apartment block roofs, insatiable streams
of supplication rise, ransack the clouds for ears

to hear their prayers. *Whine all you want*, Murray
tells himself, as if speaking to the broke artist

he half pities, half fears. *Bitch at the clocks
you can't keep up with if you want – the clocks*

*don't care,* as rain spatters on the landscape,
spreads,
        trickles down a million angled rocks.

## MIDNIGHT

Rain spatters, runs down angled rocks,
diffuses in dips. Fumes rise from the windowsill

where Viró sits, her showered hair like licked
blue cotton candy slicked across her scalp.

Hoping self-inflicted pain would nix
her sin or coffin it safely in the past,

under the shower's scalding spray
she's incised fresh lines on her thigh's inside

with an Exacto knife, and watched the blood
weep down the drain, first in streaks of red,

then pretty clouds of pink. She isn't sure
it worked.
          *At least I tried?*
                                        She can't swallow,

spits a nicotine-hued bolas onto berry leaves
two floors below.
                              Soon, Viró will harvest

the cellphones' components. Tomorrow
she'll call clients, convert inventory into cash,

repeat the steps.
                           Now she breathes. Rests.
Her inner thigh's incisions sting, as the air

outside gets damp. Viró crooks a look
at winged things circling with cups and tools

around a central tree, shedding the blood of snakes,
chasing droplets from the wounded human flattened

to the maple's bark. Streams of air flow past her,
impelling the arrangement into motion:

spirits' swords and goblets clink softly
off the corpses of their verminous victims,

off white drops of flying blood or chrism;
hinged wings lift as counterweights sink, chime

when their counterweights rise. Viró pictures it
cast in chrome and gilt, hung in an airy church

to spin its cycles till the Big One hits,
and *no regrets*, she thinks, *it's all I could have hoped.*

Viró looks north: the far shore's wooded slopes
are draped in night. Viró snaps a landscape,

texts it to her dad's old number, wonders
what she'll do when her mom comes calling

for cash… what knowledge her mother
might give, or trade for support. Virgae

toss cool raindrops across the lane and Viró
is letting them speckle her bare shins

when her phone-screen blinks with a text
from Vanessa. *Let's drive up the mountain*

it reads. *My Big died. Pretty please?*
A prank?
Viró runs downstairs, waves her empty hands

at the cam. They meet outside. Vanessa
wants to ease her claustrophobia by seeing

the universe deprived of light, restored
to its innate infinity, so both girls

ride Nessy's Echo to a gravel pit
halfway up the hills.
They sit on boulders –

share a slightly stale joint Vanessa scored
at the Manor party,
looking out across

the kingdom of the clock's abyssal lights.
Vanessa tells how Connor stood unsure

on the steel railing, his back's outline
blind to the outcrying human world

before he leaned outward, muttering words
she couldn't hear, and dropped.
*Why'd he do it?*

Vanessa asks. *Because of me?*
*No way,*
Viró says. *Not without first making sure you knew*

*he blamed you. Think they'll find a note?*
Vanessa ponders this.
*I said*, Viró

reiterates, dismayed at her own impatience,
*do you think he left a note.*
*No. I think*

*he didn't know he was going to do it*
*until he did.*
Viró's wrist flicks a rock

downhill: it rips through ferns with a sound
like an animal turning to run.
*Even maya*

*is maya*, says Vanessa. *Any notion what that means?*
*That's a Buddhist thing,* Viró says, *it means*

*nothing's real, the world's a mirage. Why?*
Vanessa weighs this philosophy

against what she knew of Connor – how
if she lay against him during a film

he'd fall asleep, wake up with a blissful smile
when the credits rolled – how he'd tunnel under

warm blankets on weekend mornings,
snuffle, grunt, pretend to be a beast

blowing raspberries on any flailing limb of hers
he caught; how when they camped

by a glacial lake, he peeled his sweaty clothes off,
plunged in with slapstick glee, to re-emerge

with genitals shrivelled as sun-dried fruit
poking fun at his own anatomy –

*That's fucked,* Vanessa says, crying, wringing
her insides dry until Viró shrugs, squeezes

a hand fondly around her friend's ankle –
but when Vanessa glances up suspiciously

she doesn't see the hungry, hurting smile
Viró used to have when they touched, but just

a friend with tender reassurance.
*Before I'm super stoned,* Vanessa sniffs,

*I need to say: when I got home, there was*
*a party at the Manor. Some folks you knew.*

*Japanese lanterns. Haigan singing French.*
*A different world than Le Crocodile,*

*more mine. That's when I cried for Connor first.*
*Crying came when I felt safe again, and*

*relief too – like I'd escaped a trap. Does that*
*make sense to you?*
Viró thinks what to say.

*Today,* she tells her former crush, *was hell.*
*But I'm almost glad. When they pulled down*

*our Clifton place, I thought I could only live*
*alone. It took a disaster like today*

*to see the goof I'd made.*
The city below
spills odd-lot photons from glass blocks.

Enough for the young women to see by
but blank in the pics they click for a joke,

post tagged #*youhadtobethere*
Where? They're
giddy with THC, halfway between

thick clouds and docks gleaming in the unseen
clockwork that ticks from ship to shore.

Pale auras emitted by the necklace of bulbs
outlining the high suspension bridge bloat

as fog surrounds them, focus again as
the mist recedes. Laughing over old times,

shedding tears for men they never knew,
two friends analyze longing and death

and art. *What's it all about?* Vanessa asks,
when Viró mentions her sculpted mobile.

*Everything*, she responds, trying to avoid
profaning her work with words.
*What's your play about?*

The gravel pops with raindrops but the pair
sit in the deluge until they're shaking –

somehow elated, taking selfies
cheek to cheek while spattered water sparkles

prismatically on screens, then race like wet cats,
slam car doors shut to hush the rain's cackle

to a chuckle.
Two hours before, fed-up cops
dragged exultant Glen through discharge, let him flop

on the station's steps.
Convenience stores
near drunk tanks retail rice wine, tax in,

for a buck ninety-nine, so Glen grinned his thanks
to the doe-eyed girl who flipped him a toonie,

and when his legs started working again,
skipped kitty-corner for 30 proof Shaoxing.

His organs of sense now humid, electric,
Glen tracks a herd of elongated beasts

toward the beach. Between sinuous necks of smoke,
he spies the sunken ocean shrunken back,

slumping citadels on the exposed sea floor
open for all comers to despoil. Desperate

to get there before the good loot's gone
Glen takes a wrong turn in the shadows,

traps himself in a waterfront cul-de-sac.
He can smell the beach but can't find a break

in the cedar hedge as alcohol filtering
from gut to bloodstream trips him into toxic shock.

He vomits a stream of acidic sick,
begins to topple. The slippery scales

of cedar twigs slither through his hands,
and on the damp ground, he releases his bladder

and bowels, fouling himself, not sleeping
but sinking, his poisoned organs ticking

down their final turns.
                                        Purple tones loom
off clouds over the kingdom's blocks. Soft bodies

move or sleep in coral cells.
                                        Restless,
the kingdom of the clock's illicit

and official fictions execute planned
exchanges of fees, services, and rents,

complete algorithmic tasks, enforce set
cycles of asset use and obsolescence.

## CLOSING TIME

Cycling through over-used and obsolete lines,
a pickup artist peacocking in a baby pink raincoat

casts his proposals over shoals of girls
that swim from closing clubs. Walking alongside

pairs or groups, he asks: *You look like experts,*
*where's the best place to go after hours?*

To passing singletons, he holds up his phone
saying: *Hey, before I call my friend back,*

*I need your feedback on what his girlfriend*
*told him.* He's tired, not set on what he labels

kino-escalation but trying from habit to hit
his daily quota of attempts.
                                        In bedside cribs

babies wake to suck from breast or bottle,
drop back to sleep and toddlers waddle

from nurseries to ask for snacks, seek someone
to read stories while they eat. Cozy

in fleece sleep sack, Larissa's scrunched up
on her pillow in a posture like a frog,

while Mehrdad gets her back to the land of Nod
by reading aloud *The Golden Key*. Glad

for something to do while he waits for news,
Mehrdad savours Victorian phrases

he reads by his phone screen's glow,
and listens for Larissa's breath to deepen,

acquire the neutrality of sleep. No rest
for Mehrdad, not while the black box stays

buried.
        No stranger to insomnia,
Mehrdad returns to the bookshelf

where copies of Yusuf's works are arrayed
like trophies beside the volumes Mary's written.

He swaps his blue-bound book of fairytales
for a *Khorda Avesta*, takes it to the balcony

where he can see the sky, find the Mah Yasht
and pray the Hymn to the Moon

while invisible servants of creation
cycle past on eternal circuits:

> *Immortals are keepers of the moon's glory.*
> *Immortals pour out its glory on the earth*
>
> *that Mazda made. And when the moon waxes*
> *in the springtime, it brings golden plants*
>
> *from the earth… give unto my grandson*
> *brightness and glory, give him health of body,*
>
> *give him the bright, the blissful abode*
> *of the holy ones.*

                                The old formulas

dive into his mind like goshawks with claws
outstretched to drive away the piles

of blackened, twitching snakes foretelling
his grandson will be born sick, afflicted

with fatal decay. Mehrdad looks out on
the bay, on the fleet of illuminated freighters

at anchor, an inverse version of the nightscape
he saw so often after Armin died,

when he stepped sleepless between buckets,
nudged blooms aside to watch twig-like larvae

twitching under the bent surface
of thickening slime. Periodic chirps, clinks

of Saena's beak on brass bars notched higher
his weary anger, till he felt a midnight urge

to toss the birdcage off the public pier,
hear its frets slice the ocean with a hiss.

Instead, each sleepless night he'd trundle down
to that dock with sour pails of flowers, dump their ooze

in the dark, let brine annihilate their broods.
Only when Armin's deathbed blooms were all

entrusted to the tide did he ask Mo
to adopt the canary, give Mehrdad

silence. *Tonight will be different,* he thinks.
*Tonight there's a future to pray for.*
Cloud gaps

glitter with stars as the night's final sobs
drip down, rippling the flipped images

of signs, buildings, lampposts and wires
that float in flooded streets. College kids

chase last buses through puddles, self-sort
into pairs of priestess and priest, their breaths

becoming spiced like sunny train tracks strewn
with jasmine: in residence rooms, these celebrants

reiterate their liturgy two by two:
*That feels good.*
                    *Yes.*
                              *Keep doing that.*
                                        *Oh, God!*

*I love you.*
            *I love you too.*
                                They clench, press
in narrow beds till stiffness turns to softness,

blood seeps ecstatically through brains. Sated,
enervated hands wipe moisture from membranes,

re-flatten matted hair. In see-through traps
of latex tubes, pools of opal goo droop.

A slippery knot midway completes
the rite. Why use these sheaths, not pills?

Pills gave these priestesses the blues, made them
hear disembodied laughter when they closed

their eyes for sleep, left them weeping in class
over old battlefields: *O war, war, war!*

they sobbed, *What's it all for?*
                                        Souls pipetted
from living skulls drip into dreams

of past exams, erotic skits, or shifts
of friend to fiend. Rainfall ticks

at the periphery of parkades, spiders and beetles
stilt-walk in microcosms, eating, being eaten;

ants carry crumbs to crannies; moths
meander on vertical columns, wings selectively

matched to concrete.
Hankering for sand to rest
his sore feet on before going home, and

light-licked waves to watch one by one collapse,
Murray traps himself in a cul-de-sac.

Bending to check the cedar hedge for a gap
shaped by dogs or kids, the smell of sickness prickles

on his tongue. *What is this?* he hisses, as his
shoes splash in a foul pool and bump on a body

prone in its own sewage. Murray swears,
then stops, squats over the still, face-down form

that in the dark reminds him of a man
who used to watch him out of mirrors.

He rubs his finger under the mucus-
blocked nose, prods Glen's neck, detects

a halting pulse. *Motherfucker*. Murray rolls him,
peers at the creased, slimy face. *Piece of shit,*

Murray calls him, *you stupid fuck*. His eyes get wet,
alone in the shadows with a half-dead drunk.

He pats his pockets for the cellphone
he left at home, he yells for help. The dead-end

stays silent, still.
No way out. Murray
snorts his tears back, hocks a loogie

on the ground. He shoves his son-of-a-butcher hands
under the slack body, feels his fingernails

scrape the putrid mud beneath.
His bad heart's pounding on his ribs

but Murray hauls Glen's flopping head
across his shoulder, strains his haunches

to stand. He feels his saddlebags of blubber
sag. Drips of vomit mixed with sewage

slip down his back as Murray staggers
up the sidewalk toward sounds of traffic,

croaking huskily for help.
                                        Wondering
if anyone would care if spirits snatched them up

into purplish clouds
                                down flooded streets
the one-man bands of the lonely go. At

each one's heels, shadows cast by streetlights
chase, swing past like clock hands while replacements

grow unseen behind, match their models' pace
and move into pole position to overtake

the plodding, lonely feet they race through
puddles slicked with gasoline and soap.

## THE WATCH

Puddles slicked with gasoline and soap
split light into orange and purple: radiation spilled

from lit foyers dulls the moon to a dim circle, effaces
all but a few stars, faint as flecks of chalk

on sidewalks.
In hospice care, Glen's father
wakes – each point of light or contact with skin

a torture were it not for the IV's analgesic drip.
Clucking in his throat, Don calls his wife

from the couch nearby. A cup is brought.
His wife's older than he thought, her hands

have a tremor he's forgotten. Past speaking,
he sucks gelatinized water, grins his thanks,

then settles back to rest. Leena tries to sleep, but
the silence feels too thick – Don's ragged breath

is missing. A machine bleeps, a red light shines
to announce Don's heart has stopped, his pulse

paused. She bumps the red button; some nurses
come.
There's suddenly no rush, nothing left

to help in the failed flesh. The self's holdfast
has broken from its brain and the buoyant

ribbons are circling up.
Leena breathes.
*It's done. It's finally done.*
She will reproach

no one. Should she telephone their girls or Ken,
so late at night? How will she contact Glen?

Was Don too hard on them? On her?
She's in no mood to judge, sensing her release

like a lull between waves. His creased skin
is still. His wrecked engine's cooling down.

She leaves the nurses to their work,
carefully climbs down rubberized stairs

to ground level. She prefers to phone
her children where only the living can hear.

Near intake, Leena leans against the wall
before she makes her calls. It's raining again.

When the ER doors slide open, she sees
the eaves' waterfalls splash in frantic lines

like a kind of linear static. Pregnant
women arrive with men or mothers

or lovers in tow – sick kids drowse in laps –
a lady Leena's own age apologizes

to a nurse for falling down at home.
An ambulance drives up outside, raindrops

hopping on the hood. Paramedics gurney in
the patient: Leena sees Glen's rank head joggle

with vibrations from the wheels, repeating,
as it always did, her husband's heavy lashes,

her husband's heavy chin.
What persists
as we tick past two? Sirens

that chase calamity from scene to scene?
Grey mice between the tracks of robot-driven

trains? Undergrads drinking in cramped dorms
after finishing exams? Those who work

in darkness only half believe our sunlight
laws still stand. Up late, franchisees tweak

accounting entries to bilk franchisors
with falsified reports; church-goers urge

each other to invest in a Ponzi scheme.
Such exchanges animate the kingdom

of the clock, but one by one their trades
complete, blink out like eyes. The city sleeps.

Over the rooftop kvetching of raindrops
Feng attends to the Foley effects

of Meghan's clumsy wanderings downstairs,
her abrupt swinging and slamming of cupboard doors,

the simian cackling of the perched owl
somewhere near. Accepting rest won't come

till she confirms or debunks her guess,
Feng gets up, wriggles into an old raincoat

by the door, fiddles with her wedding ring.
Her husband had a knack for extracting

Meghan's secrets. But he died in a Mong La
rejuvenation spa, his onshore assets

seized by Beijing rivals higher up
the food chain.
                    She creeps through sheets of rain

to a basement window, sets her feet
in a weed-grown garden bed, and stoops

to peer inside. Terrified of offending
Meghan's aversion to surveillance, Feng

prostrates herself on hands and knees, twists
painfully to watch what transpires within:

Meghan paces in black t-shirt and panties,
rooting through long-stored boxes for dolls

and lumps of polished amethyst to array
on side tables in what, Feng supposes,

are meant to be shrines. Each centres on
one of the Russian dolls Meghan once

obsessively popped apart and reassembled,
round which the stones and lesser figurines

are set in rows. Mid-wander, Megan stops
in front of her hallway mirror – lifts

her shirt's hem to pose with hands framing
a heart-shape on the tummy bump that juts

where her womb sits
                                        and Feng
feels a lever she's been holding shut pull free –

feels her world displaced by a newer world
that reverses the old one's purposes and rules.

While Meghan preens, strokes the skin
behind which she imagines gemlike cells

splitting into runnels of opal
and carnelian swells, Feng lies flat

on the damp soil, allows the peens
of raindrops to beat and burst upon her

as she smiles as she has not smiled for years. Mud
splashes in her mouth, a stem invades her ear

but it all only makes her gladder. The taste
of unexpected love is in her teeth –

towards new burdens her labour's earned
the capability to meet, her weeping heart

goes leaping like a salmon, gulping sweet
currents whose cataclysmic tastes

transform her synapses: *What next,*
she asks herself, *what will Meghan let me do?*

*May I give my grandchild all I have, and*
*all I'll ever have?*
On Viró's third-hand couch,

the friends are disassembling phones: Vanessa
slowly removing screws and shells, Viró

peeling with practiced hands components
from their slots, securing them in labelled ziplocks

for resale, scattering waste parts and cases
out the window, into blackberry bushes

in the alley below. They're both stoned
and Vanessa catches herself sometimes

screwing clamshells shut she'd just pried open,
humming along as Nanci Griffith sings

from the Bluetooth tube she brought in
from her car.
Viró pauses to watch

Vanessa work – to savour the sight of
her face purified with focus. Guilt blending

with pleasure, she recalls fantasies
unhappily entertained years before:

the two of them alone and high, Vanessa
craving comfort as much as Viró craved her –

only now, she's not so sure what kind of lure
it was that hunched behind her craving

for closeness, and when she tells Vanessa
how she stole these devices, her friend

absolves her, dismisses the significance
of theft, by saying:
*Everyone makes mistakes.*

A simple truth, and Viró thanks her for it.
But if Viró's truthful with herself, is "mistake"

the word she'd use? Rent came due;
she didn't pay. How many warnings did she

burn unopened, smoking on her windowsill? As her
designs for the sculpture grew more complex,

she knew – it soothed her to think about it –
in a pinch, she could always steal. Can you call

your backup plan "mistake" when it's followed
through?
The song ends. Vanessa lets YouTube
stop, ignores thumbnails of country hits

tiled on her laptop screen like cards. Viró clicks
a pearly case onto her own phone, strokes

its printed peachy roses. *What if you run*
*into the one you stole it from*, asks Nessy,

and Viró shrugs. *I'll give it back.*
In the pause
rain batters bramble leaves like drumskins

in the alleyway outside.
A breeze spins
Viró's mobile crucifix, its elements

clinking when they contact, voiced like
a tilted rainstick. Viró stops sorting phone parts

to sketch Vanessa's concepts for pop-up
scenery and props, Viró's own thoughts

for folding costumes where flash metamorphoses
might elicit gasps.
Tonal phrases programmed

into flightpaths draw the girls' attention
to the sculpture cycling around the ceiling,

and Vanessa comments on its graces, its kind
and vindictive shapes. Viró did not mean

to give her figures these affects, but each
creature's charged with something – gratitude,

reluctance, or detachment in their task
of chasing drops of grace. Their system floats,

orbits a bleeding man and tree half-concealed
by their complexities.
Discussing

meanings and feelings they half-perceive,
both miss that brief epoch of innocence

when they were newly friends.
Feng washes mud
from her hair in the ensuite shower, and wonders

how far Meghan might transgress with a baby
as her hostage:
*What drugs, what chances will she take*

*with foetal cells as they assemble?*
Her fears
don't cancel out a hope she's formed

from sentiments she sensed in Meghan's shrines
where maternal dolls concealing children

safe inside were given pride of place,
the exuberance with which Meghan spun

before the mirror. Feng hopes for the best, but knows
she can't count on Meghan's sobriety

while open markets downtown trade
in every substance she takes to self-medicate.

*But what if we left the city?* Feng asks
the humid air, the splashing spray: *Sell the house*

*and learn to love horse country? Magpies?*
*Quiet?* Feng recalls her girlhood in the hills

under the star's calendar, before
her parents sent her to the clock's kingdom

for school: the blue peaks she'd kick at,
backstroking with her god-like grandmother

across the lake.
Feng knows lives don't alter
through arithmetics of pros and cons

but only when the desperate will leaps
instinctively, and Feng's pleased to feel

the outline of a plan emerge, as if arranged
offstage, and wheeled into the light –
                                        she'll quit

practice, list the house and buy
nothing grand. A clearing at road's end,

with hens for Meghan to guard from mink and coyote,
with cherry trees to pick. A produce stand

by the highway – even just a dropbox
with a jar. Woods to walk in. A lake wherein

to swim. A barn for nanny goats to milk, for stables
if the grandchild likes to ride.
                                        Her choice made,

a plan of action forms around finding realtors
to hire, which files to sell to whom,

what referral fees to charge. Feng wipes
the steamed-up mirror with a washcloth,

inspects her parched, pale, thin-skinned frame – hopes
she can tease nineteen years of strength from joints

and bones long unmaintained.
                                        Outside, her owl
takes flight unseen – scanning lawns and lanes

for prey as it tries to retrace its way
to valley fields it never meant to leave.

*Will we miss the kingdom when we move,* Feng
wonders as she settles into bed, *like*

*the citadel, like the stronghold it sometimes*
*seems? Or will we recall only its decay*

*and dereliction, like those abandoned*
*sailboats rotting slowly in the bay?*

## INTEMPESTA

Enoch's boat rocks slowly in the bay,
disused sails decaying in their shrouds. He stirs,

roused by a dull drumbeat, thinks the Port
is calling him to work. *Tump-thummity-tump*

the rhythm runs… the sound of something soft
bumping on the hull. Headlamp strapped on,

Enoch ventures into the floating darkness
of the deck, picks up his boat hook to detach

what's snagged. Bracing his knees in the bow pulpit,
he looks down – sees the protean fins and wings

ocean derives from light beams and lower down,
darker forms beneath the prow.
                                        Clothed limbs

fluctuate in the current below him,
legs kick lazily against the hull.

With the boathook, Enoch drags the body aft
till he can reach over the gunwale, load

one dripping limb at a time into the cockpit
while against his back, the tiller ticks like a stuck

seconds hand, its nylon stays slightly slackened
by the rain.
                    Frigid from the sea floor, the corpse

cancels out heat like an ice cube, makes
the night's atmosphere cool as a cave. Breath

turns to mist in Enoch's headlamp's beam
as he bends down to examine features

puffed as if just lifted from a pillow,
glassy eyes wide and blue as April windows.

Checking pockets for ID, Enoch finds
a bricked iPhone, a Tiffany ring box,

and within that a fat wet diamond ring.
Enoch sighs.
*So.*
*Was this a pre- or post-*

*proposal leap?*
*Who knew about this ring?*
*The would-be fiancée?*
*The drowned man's folks?*

Enoch knows to report the corpse, wait for
harbour police to buzz by and bag it

but – *This ring's a bitter last supper*
*for near and dear to share,* he thinks. *Suicide's*

*sour enough without a Tiffany solitaire*
*and the guilt and blame it brings.* He considers

pocketing the bling, but a moment's thought
of having to hawk it makes him ill. He checks

dead eyes, dead face and hands, recoils from their
abyssal chill.
*Rules are rules,* he wants to tell

the man's departed self, *at least for men like me*
*who live on the periphery... but still.*

*I don't want to call the cops on what you've done.*
*Why not a sea burial, clean and cheap? Already*

*you feel like a possession of the deep.*
Enoch clicks off his lamp to exit the jurisdiction

of clocks and laws. From the cabin he fetches
fishing weights and slips them with dead phone

and boxed ring into the corpse's chino pockets.
The city's surplus efflorescence reflects

off convex corneas so Enoch presses
rubbery eyelids shut until they stick.

To avoid the man's black Nike high-tops
keeping dead feet afloat, Enoch slips

them from soaking socks, flips them off the stern,
hears them splash. He eases the dripping limbs

overboard, feels them drop away, as if the wild tide
were sucking them down.
                                        Enoch knows nothing

but pity for those who love this young man
as the young are always loved, and that the sea

will ebb till dawn, towing its acquisitions west.
Shaking off the cold the corpse exuded, Enoch

climbs back into his bunk's nest of blankets,
and quickly falls asleep.
                                        Brine clammy on his skin,

Enoch swims through dreams of an underwater
morgue, stripping ficus from rock coffins

and kelp-stipes from lips of urns. Eels of sunlight
oscillate through floating detritus above

where he rushes, rushes from one task
to the next, knowing he must be done before

the sun comes up or drown.

Viró tiptoes

for her bathroom, afraid to wake Vanessa

who's tucked in on the couch. She freezes –
retreats on hearing shallow gasps, glimpsing

the cyclical dip and thrust of hands and hips
animating the bedclothes. Viró giggles,

recalling from their days as roommates
how Vanessa would do this when she couldn't sleep

and Viró pretended not to see. Burning
to pee, Viró lifts her window, steps out

on the sill. With lights off behind her,
she hikes her t-shirt, feeling like one of those

grotesques sculptors used to place
too high on cathedrals to be seen.

She squats and pisses over the alley like a bird,
hears it patter on the blackberry plants

below. *It just rained,* she reasons,
*It'll rain again.*

A thought comes to her:

*Could I drop my creatures out the window*
*for Nessy to catch midair, shuttle safe*

*to her Manor?* No, it's too dark to see
and she remembers from tossing frisbees

in the park how inept Vanessa is at catching things.
*But what if Nessy held a net like a fireman?*

She pictures her friend lunging among
the thorny canes as plaster shapes plummet,

shatter into shards that scatter in the dark.
She shakes her head. An owl's silent outline

glides down the alley, so close she sees
its feathers troubled by the wind.
Virό's lived

too long alone, she knows, lost touch with how
tractable most problems are. It's not too late

to switch tack, she thinks: to beg for a room
in Nessy's commune, share studio space –

draw closer to the living.
Before she climbs
back into bed, she wipes windowsill grit

from her soles with a ripped Kleenex; shuts
the sash window; smirks at her outline

on the pane when she hears the couch-springs crunch
as Vanessa's pleased hips tip sideways

to sleep.
Behind condemned shopfronts, strobes
hyphenate rooms of ravers. Chemically

in love on MDMA with every
painted face and DayGlo fingernail

they see, girls fresh from proms evade crude hints
to step upstairs where a thicker beat throbs,

where men wait to fiddle with petals, probe
deeper for nectar. In taffeta hued

like roses or tulips, debs seek secret exits
behind loose sheets of plywood, clink in heels

down scaffolds and dial dads for rides, as cabs
with signs turned off race past, rushing Johns

to corners frequented by fares' favourites
or showcase zones where self-marketing

girls, boys, or girlboys cluster, so customers
can window-shop the wares they lust for.

Leeward of walls in vacant lots, streetwalkers
take breaks to swap warnings, sympathy,

and fables of what's to come:
                                        *Last time you cried?*
*When my mom died.*
                                *You gotta be strong, way*

*stronger than they think you are.*
                                        *Aren't we still*
*women? Ain't we beautiful?*
                                        Playing poker

at the casino, Mark holds back from scratching
his itchy beard, knowing that's his tell.

Another nut low. Since the dealer who looked
like Coral's doppelgänger left, he's drawn slop

and his rivals have gone cryptic –
his grey eyes can't read if they're delighted

with their hands or drunk. Mark's dizzy,
even his memory's on the fritz – he can't recall

what cards were dealt last hand, or when the dealer
last swapped decks. He can't quit when he's so far

behind, but knows he's flying blind
as the lean, chin-strapped dealer shuffles,

flips, dispenses miracles and misses
with pitiless rapidity. *There goes the dentist,*

Mark hears Coral saying when he folds,
*There goes our Cancun trip,* when his bluff's

called. *There goes this month's mortgage,* when his straight
turns out a heartbreaker. *I'm no fish,*

*I'm good at this.* Trying to stay suave, he snags
a chill martini from a passing tray and

though his stack is dwindling, Mark tips
the waitress with a princely chip. He sips

syrup from the conical cup, pictures
Coral waiting under a spotlight near the bar,

wearing a snug fuchsia dress slit down the back
like an ambiguous Bond girl, who could be

an allied spy, or double agent femme fatale.
Black hairs astray from her beehive restrain

a coppery inner light; smooth olive skin
shows in the slit that dips to her sacrum.

In this fantasy she's anxious, dismissive.
*Show her you were right,* his sickness prompts him,

*Showtime.* Mark knows he's running out of time –
knows each loss shrinks his odds another inch.

*Go for the kill,* he tells himself, *clinch a pot,*
*cash out a winner.*
Bodies softly fall

through Vanessa's dreams holding cups and knives,
beating moth-like, bat-like, bird-like wings

above black waters. More chimeras boat
on the glossy calm in sneaker-shaped

canoes, deflecting silver-rimmed waves
north and south as finned and whiskered paddles

steer them west. Crabs scrabble between layers
of *cuir bouilli* – ribbon-thin snakes slither

through rows of stone grommets
and sample the downdraft with golden tongues.

Waves chop with a repeating phrase:
*What's it all for? What's it for?* And she's

appalled, trying to fly home on flaccid wings
to prairies where no one smells the sea

while a skeletal hand yanks on her shoulder,
shaking her from the sky.
*Wake up, Nessy,*

*I need your help.* Viró stands over her,
holding a roll of fishing line.
*What's wrong?*

Viró brings Vanessa to the bedroom,
leans out the window, points bandaged index

at where an old power pole is cabled
to the building's brick.
*If I tie a creature*

*on the string,* Viró says, *I could toss it*
*across that cable, lower it down to you.*

*You could unsling it, pack it in the Echo*
*while I reel the string back up, tie on*

*the next. Could you do that?*
*Could I?*
She's too tired to answer yes or no.
*Let's try.*

Fentanyl flowing into Mary's spine
doesn't block the pain but occludes her objection

to it. As the boy moves (pain by pain)
through her pelvis, she cries for fear the strain

will detach his unmoored organs, pare
away his life on life's doorstep. Her fear

abstracts her from the Pitocin-sped tempo
of her pains, the paper johnny gown she wears,

makes her hallucinate winged numina
Yusuf's mother used to pray to – *fravashi*

who portion out creation's grace. She sees them
circle the room to a nursery tune, grips

Yusuf's hand and screams – spies an immortal
corresponding to her son as her hips splay

till the hinges crack – feels mysterious muscles
flex, propel her first-born son through

blinding blood into the light. Stamped on each cell
the sacred image shines but by some glitch

of genes or growth, infant organs
like slippery balloons and ropes slop

from a fleshy cleft left open in his chest.
The boy is beautiful in his mess, wounded

but not doomed, his organs pink and purple
with life – the doctors joke as they check

each healthy link. Yusuf weeps with relief
and gratitude as he clutches Mary's hand.

She smiles at her son through tears and sweat,
lying torn, triumphant on the bed. She senses

the spirits who helped are dog-tired too,
suddenly wobbly, slower in their circuits,

sacred cups and sabres heavy in their hands.
As nurses trolley the plastic-wrapped boy

and Mary down hallways, Yusuf watches
for obstacles while Mary scans

her baby's face and listens to him scream.
She alone can hear how he's in agony

not only with the unhealed split that burns
along his nerves but craving for her touch

and smell and voice, his newborn need for love.
Under white lights, gloved hands place each organ,

lay living tubes in loops, seal the schism's lips
with plastic. This child will be nurtured drip

by drip through tubes for months, while natural means
of life accept their functions, but in a year,

when he's a terror throwing things from heights
to watch them break, Mary's fingertip will tap

his scar, awed by how small the gap
through which her whole love nearly slipped.

Through cold holes between life and sleep,
Murray flops on the cot in his revamped panic room.

His throat feels swollen and sore, his cold rolls
of blubber slouch. Even soaped and scrubbed,

Murray can't stop smelling the mess he found –
putrid fluids that soaked deep into his pores,

infused his body hair and epidermis
with indelible odours while a shrieking siren

took forever to arrive. *Did that shitbag live?*
*We never last long on the street.* He's afraid to sleep,

afraid of recurring nightmares that bring
bilked investors galloping on all fours,

mouths wide with yellow teeth like the cattle dogs
who chased him when he was small. As those dreams

near their crescendo he always hears
the squeals, smells the feral panic of pigs

spastic on the slaughtering floor. He wishes
he could call Inez upstairs to share her warmth

but he's made that mistake before – knows
he can't rest in a woman's arms without

creating expectations he's determined
not to meet.
*What's it all for,* Murray moans,

*if I can't sleep?* Rolling on his front,
he lets his gut relax, the soft skin

of his snake's gullet slouch. He starts to sense
his brothers' reproachful tones, repels them

with thoughts of his own prestigious sons.
Exploring schemes to see his grandkids

without their mothers' knowing, he also loves
and is lonely, falling finally asleep.

Where moonlight purifies a patch of cloud,
Mehrdad focuses his eyes, trying to soak

from the sky enough lumens to keep
awake, exhale again the lunar prayer. Pressed

in his pocket against the rail, his phone
pulses, stirring vibrations through the barrier's alloy

to where his elbows rest. With shivering fingers,
Mehrdad sets down the *Khorda Avesta*,

toggles an icon to accept his son's call,
to be told a boy was born belonging to

the light of day and not the grave. Mehrdad
hears his son's voice dripping with relief,

with sorrow for Mary's pain while their son's pain
lasts. *A miracle,* says Yusuf.
                                                Both know

some prayers are heard and some refused, but the boy
will live to see sun and moon – walk at one,

talk at two, stack blocks, hear tales of heroes
and tricksters read aloud, laugh at Peppa Pig.

Yusuf turns to logistics, says he'll rush back
as soon as Mary's had a chance to rest.

*No need,* Mehrdad interrupts. *I've settled in.*
*I'll keep the divô lit until you bring the baby home.*

Yusuf thanks his father, trying not to let show
his surprise.
*A joy for me,* says Mehrdad,

*and, Yusuf, I've been thinking,* he continues,
working up to the wish that's rooted in his mind

this night: *Mary and you need time to write.*
*You'll need a nanny. That means four bedrooms:*

*a house. I don't have much ability*
*to help unless I sell my place, but then – there's*

*your down payment. I could sleep anywhere,*
*help herd the kids. I'd be the cheapest nanny,*

*if the worst.*
Taken aback, Yusuf thanks him
for the offer but won't commit – *Talk soon,*

he says, which Mehrdad knows is code for
*I'll talk with Mary before saying more.*

*I could help,* Mehrdad persists. *And don't you think*
*the boy will want a dog?*
*Thanks, Dad. Love you.*
*Let's talk soon.*
Both know how automatic
and welcome such arrangements would have been

if Armin had lived, and Mehrdad died instead.
They say goodnight.
As Armin insisted he do,

even when her skin lay like a stained sheet
around her skeleton, Mehrdad thanks the beings

who administer their creator's blessings
from a stillness behind the clouds.

He foresees weeks of strain, of Yusuf
and Mary holding vigil in the NICU until

the boy comes home, but he's thankful
for more Peppa Pig, more bearing Larissa

down aisles of night – more chances to exchange
his loneliness for the chores of love.
The casino's sign

shines peacock light on the packed parkade
where Mark can't find his pickup. Blue-green

radiation limns his likenesses in side-mirrors,
reminds him he's leaving a loser.

Mark thumbs his fob, but there's no beep,
no throb of headlights flashing on and off.

His sickness flicks a thought across his mind:
*What if I go back – back to the table and win?*

Near the casino's entrance, ATMS
hover in a pool of light. *I'm being tested*

Mark chuckles (pores beneath his beard oozing
psychoactive oils). *To see if I've got guts*

*enough to win.* Behind his silver eyes,
Mark's soul looks out, licks its gums, lets malware

pilot him from the peacock parkade's glare
back to a spotlit ATM. Adanac's

overdraft is still untapped, held back
for payroll. He drains it, dreaming it'll double

by dawn – imagines Coral
amazed in the morning at how their account

plumped up. Nerves thrilled, heart pounding
to the malware's signals, he watches bills

rattle in the plastic tray, crisp as seagulls' quills.
*This takes real guts,* Mark hears the virus say.

*Quitters' money never wins, winners' money
never quits. What's it all for, if you can't*

*wager when it's finally your turn to win?*
Out east the bank's unsleeping neural net detects

his withdrawal, assesses it to guess
if Adanac's being robbed, if an imposter

cloned Mark's card and PIN. But no – the algorithm
tracks the pattern, can predict what happens next:

payroll cheques will bounce, Mark's guys will walk,
his business fail. He'll siphon from Coral

her savings. He'll beg, he'll borrow, sue, blame
bank errors for ISFs. When Coral

locks him out, he'll start to steal and lose
that money too. In Mark's hands, the fresh cash

feels unreal – evanescent as sights passing
at night through shoals of dreaming skulls.

## BEFORE WAKING

At night, the shells of dreamers' selves
crack – spilled contents mix and spark. As quick

as brains give them being, scenes substantiate
and sublimate, come alive with light,

fade back to non-being. Sleepers are chased
in sequences from TV shows or

experience the pangs of a broken heart
screaming its secret urges, unguessed at

and unwelcomed by the waking. Retirees
re-enact commutes, scramble to catch flights

from labyrinthine airports; teachers fail
to decode symbols they know should be simple;

surgeons' fingers are scorched in furnaces
hidden under spotless skin.
Vanessa watches

each grey blotch above her brighten to bone-white,
swing pendulum-wise as it drops through the dark.

Each oscillation's extreme goes *clack* or *click*
as hinged parts flip forth and back

and each creature is almost in her fingers' grips
before she perceives its birdlike, angelic,

piscatory features, makes out pairs of wings
reminiscent of various taxa,

limbs that end in human hands and toes
or terminate in hoofs and claws transformed

to fishhooks, sickles, cups, and ulus.
As she receives each plaster chimera

she snips the opalescent twenty-pound test
each hangs by and stacks the statuettes

in her Echo's hatch, wrapped in blankets
with hinged wings pinned back. She counts them

as they come: *sixty-six, sixty-seven,*
She wonders: *is this what Connor's mother meant*

*by even the maya is maya?* She thinks *That's silly,*
flicks the thought into chill oblivion. When

last of all the wounded man and tree
are packed, each rat and snake in a separate sack,

Viró exits with a thumbs up, arrives
at the car carting nothing but her satchel

full of phone parts, and in her anorak
pockets, reservoirs of plaster teardrops.

She plops into Vanessa's passenger seat,
beside the woman she once wanted

to love or be loved by. *Got all you need?*
Vanessa asks. Viró nods, looking back

at spirits piled higgledy-piggledy in the hatch:
*This is an escape,* she jubilates. *All*

*that matters is we make it out,*
feeling like
she'd made artificial tail feathers unfold

from her heels and remiges array her wrists,
as if she was a hobbled prisoner making

jailbreak on ash-blue wings through altitudes
midway between the sun's uncompromising arc

and the slap and splash of wardening
waves.
Slithering eels of bedrock ridden

by the city slip from high-pressure clasps,
crash loose for a few inches –

impact, rattle our stacks of glass and steel.
Shockwaves stretch and compress rubber insets

in streets and bridges before they dissipate,
unnoticed by any citizens except

a few in upper floors of skyscrapers,
who feel their buildings flinch as in a wind,

quail in the drifting mist as if afraid.
The sea shimmies smoothly in its saddle

and vessels departing port sense nothing,
blaring their air horns for open water.

Enoch tucks the next ship in its foggy nest,
looks forward to painting after he gets

some rest, to seeing Samson after school.
*I'll do better today,* he muses, *I'll tell him*

*things he's never heard before.* Glass buoys
click in the harbour, sweep needled boughs

of arc-light at diving shapes of cormorants and seals.
All water is wild. What's this wilderness want?

Flushed contact lenses float west like jellyfish,
joining the kingdom's flotilla of used face masks,

cracked bins, and nets jettisoned by boats
out sifting the sea for fish. What are they

destined for? A litter gyre? Another shore?
Devices are clammed shut or belly-down

by bedsides now, pings and stimuli
silenced. What's the kingdom's purpose

if not to let us sleep, blot out news items,
notifications pushed to phone screens by

addictive apps?
Jack lifts his thick suitcase
off the luggage carousel. Landed safely

in Suvarnabhumi Airport, he's breezed
through customs. *No warrant's been issued*

*yet*, he thinks, telescoping out the handle,
rolling the luggage behind him until he finds

a bench to plop on. Safely seated,
he switches his wingtips for flip-flops, packs

his wool sports coat into his suitcase
before leaving this air-conditioned haven.

With sleeves rolled up, collar unbuttoned,
Jack strolls on, sandals pit-patting between bare heels

and floor tiles red and green, arranged
to evoke the cobra's spectacled hood,

do homage to Nong Nguhao, the Cobra Swamp
from which this airport rose. In arrivals,

Jack sees friends hug, tour guides welcoming
their guests.
*Where's Kitty?* Jack's gripped by fear;

Kitty should be here. By now, the banks
have all been closed for hours, and Kitty's tasks

fulfilled, the gold re-sold for stocks and bonds,
the rented truck and guards paid off –

unless some tragedy befell; double-crossed
by the hired guards, or worse, a trap, arrest –

Jack's phone buzzes.
*Just parked*, texts Kitty.
Jack sends back a thumbs-up, heartbeat slowing

back to normal as he trudges alongside
a polychromatic statue of good

and wicked godlings hoisting the scaly
waves of an endless snake. As he exits

the airport through sliding doors, the night's heat
hits his wide face like a splash of blood.

He walks heavily across a footbridge to the parkade,
starting to sweat, annoyed at the curb

to find no Kitty, no Evoque. It's too hot
to walk. Jack stands tall, scans the parking lot.

Other passengers mill around, but Jack's been
a big man long enough to know he's not

easy to miss in a crowd. He spots
his hot pink SUV across the lot,

and cringes – *It does look like a crook's car.*
He waves to Kitty who sits behind

the windshield, and sighs behind his smile
as he lumbers off the curb, his bag's wheels

jarring on the pavement when they bump down.
Kittisak starts the engine, but lets it idle, leaves

the lights off and the car in park for a pause
that puzzles Jack until he hears his name

called in a child's voice. It's a boy –
or girl, perhaps – on a Suzuki bike.

A helmet's tinted glass conceals the face.
There's something familiar in the voice –

something pleasing in the kid's shape that Jack
can't place. Vapour lamps flicker overhead.

The tween on the dirt bike lifts a pistol
and shoots. Jack tries to duck and run but he's

a big man, not easy to miss. Kittisak
watches it happen. The hillock of fallen man

quivers with each bullet's blow as the dirt bike
scoots alongside, gun barrel barking

until the chamber clicks. The slim killer
bends down, adroitly pulls Jack's wallet, phone,

and passports out, slips off his rose-gold watch,
lets the thick wrist drop. When the two-stroke

engine revs, and studded tires bump across
the outstretched hand, another shudder moves

through the heap of flesh. Then nothing. Stillness.
Kittisak's pulse slows from its manic pace.

He puts his car in gear. Tooling toward the exit,
he admires the softness of its upholstery,

the quality of its engineering as never before.
He's never heard of Omniopticon

and never will. He flicks the stereo on:
Palmy's plaintive but reassuring voice

begins to croon. It's a long drive home
to the house that's finally his own.
Glen floats

in the loneliness of his hospital bed –
freezes when he hears linoleum squeak,

sees his sister Donna shifting her weight
from hip to hip, with Ken behind her,

arms akimbo. *Don't talk,* she says. *The tube*
*they pumped you out with got you good.* Glen

coughs as he tries to grin. She smirks: *It's good*
*to see you too.* Holds up a key. *Remember this?*

Of course he does. The shed in Donna's yard
her husband fixed up as a home for him.

Glen lets his head roll back, the shame
still hot from how he would slyly watch

his oldest niece walk back and forth past windows.
*We'll build a fence,* she says, *Give you your space,*

*and Ken's got a new build in the Props, says*
*he could really use your help.*
*Roofing weather?*

Glen hopes, looking over Donna's shoulder
at Ken, at purple clouds in a simple sky.

*Dad just died,* Ken says, *and Mom was calling us*
*to come when you rolled in beside her.*

*Mom said it was a gift, Glen,* Donna adds.
*We're all so glad you're back.*
She stubs the key

in his palm. Grieving his soul's sickness,
Glen pokes back the key, points up at Ken.

Ken points at himself. *You'd rather live with me?*
He laughs. *Christ, Glen. Yeah, of course.*
Donna wipes

her face clean, smiles, and leaves. *How many times*
*can you go home and fuck it up,* Glen wonders,

*before they let you die?* There's more
forgiveness in this life than he can stand.

Ken kneels beside the bed, sandwiches Glen's hand
between his own.
*Mum's moving in too,* says Ken.

*Think we could take care of her together?*
Glen freezes up, then nods. Ken bows his head.

Glen knows he's praying –
*It's such a waste,*
Glen thinks. *If I'll always relapse, go back*

*to sin, isn't it a sin to let them try*
*to trust me again? Is one summer in the garden*

*worth showing them again how deep the gangrene goes?*
Glen remembers how good it feels to eat

with Ken and Donna and their mom, with David
and the kids, to share the sour atmosphere

of cleaning fish on the spit with Ken, slinging guts
for eagles to catch mid-air, to work on rooftops

with the smell of metal, glue and cedar
warming in the sunlight. Glen turns his head

to the wall, but Ken kneels by his side
till his brother's asleep.
In the night's neutral deeps

rodents crawl through reefs of litter, tantalize
the peevish owl that floats above.

Lobster-like skunks scoop grubs from moss –
on one slant roof a raccoon claws his rival

until it plummets, crunches down
concrete steps three floors below. Crows quarrel

over the day's detritus; gulls squawk
from soggy housetops, glaucous blobs

in the pre-dawn dark. *Impartial gods*
*of birds and fish,* implore the hermits

of the park, *let us refresh ourselves*
*like simple beasts. Let natural purposes*

*be revived –*
Mark's pickup cools in the driveway
tick by tick. Coral pads out barefoot, sucking

a Virginia Slim, then tossing it aside.
She slides onto the bench seat in her kimono,

thumps the door shut so the cab's lights
fade. Mark bows his head. Coral sucks in

a lungful of air – balls her fists and screams.
Eyes grey as rocks, Mark's ready for a fight,

but his wife's been angry all night – she's done now
with anger and in the dark, her hand is there

to stroke his tawny beard, the jaw beneath.
At her soft touch, he breaks: his own breath

abrasive in his throat. She's crying too.
He tells her what he's done. She nods. She knew.

She's mad, but grateful he came home at all.
What now? *I know what happens next,* she says.

*Some A/R's due. We tell the guys they can split it.*
*They won't all quit. We'll sell the house*

*while the market's hot. Save up, rebuild.*
*We did it once. We'll work real hard. I still*

*love you.* She scares herself by adding
*I'm not afraid.* Mark looks up amazed

into her loneliness and what he sees
reaches into him and wrenches something

loose. *Lord in Heaven.* He grins. *O Lordy.*
He leans out and her fingers clutch, tug

his shoulders tight against her breasts
on the bench seat of the truck.
Vague nimbi

shelter ski hills, splashed with the false dawn
of halogen lamps. The world's half bared,

half buried in darkness. Stockbrokers tip wired waiters
at all-night Denny's. Pre-market quotes

on Bloomberg terminals tick green for up,
tock red for down, but Murray's still sunk

in a dream of scammed investors chasing him
through cul-de-sacs and cedar hedges, claws scratching

on sidewalks behind him. Finding a scaffold
by a half-built house, he scrambles up its rungs,

leaves the frenzied pack of cattle-dogs below.
He steps onto a roof's rim, looking south

towards the sea. Suspended pearls still glow
above the bridge, and massive ships float

in their own lamplight.
A staple gun
is heavy in his hand and in the dim pre-dawn

he notices the roof's black felt is pock-marked
with bales of shakes. He hears the twang

of a bale-strap snipped, and looks around. A lanky man
with long black hair bends over the loose cedar,

sorting by size. *Careful of that air hose*,
he says, *The main risk on a roof's the edge,*

*but tripping's next.*
*Aren't we clipping in?* asks Murray.
*Up to you*, Glen gently replies, *but personally*

*I like to feel free.* In Murray's dream
they work for hours, placing ranks of cedar,

tacking shakes to straps, snapping chalk lines,
ripping angles with skill saws at every hip.

As the air warms, it's steeped with smells of tar,
aerosols of cedar and spruce. On breaks,

the two chug salty lemonade from plastic jugs.
*My dad's old recipe,* Glen explains, wiping drips

from his heavy chin. Washed westward
with the sunlight, strange creatures float

across the sky on bone-white wings,
administering assays with blades and bowls,

announcing proofs that certify them pure.
*It isn't true!* says Murray to spirits who stare

back with discs shaped like the eyes of owls
or salmon,
                    *I've done bad things!* Glen keeps working

as the spirits pass, selects more shakes to lay.
*Me too,* he whispers back. *Me too.*
                                                        Lamplight

through balcony curtains spreads, spills across
Samson and Anna tucked together

on the couch. Samson's awake, watching
bright shapes puppeted on the plaster surface

but pretending to sleep to keep his mother's arm
around him. Anna dreams of ideograms

formed in salty seas by fish and seals,
in sweetened air by moths and birds. Her alarm

ticks down in sync with a million other clocks
but
    her fellow citizens still dream: livid,

chilled – the kingdom's myriads of eyes still
lidded. No love or loneliness left. No self.

No selves. Specks of impersonal worry
flicker in and out of being, ready to fuse,

irradiate sleeping souls with sensations
of air and cloth on skin, the shapes

of seagulls slicing the shapelessness of mist.
By sand banks, Coho and Pinks drink

the full river's flush through gills – until
they recognize the scent of their nurseries

and surge upstream, undulant salmon singing
like homesick sailors:

> *We remember, we remember! Clocks*
> *have revived our memories of rocks*
>
> *ticking downstream; crayfish feeding; sleek*
> *dippers with witchy eyes; a heron's beak*
>
> *aflame with amber light; beetles with picks*
> *for fists leaning out hungrily from sticks.*
>
> *We remember clams and scat on the backs*
> *of beaverdams; caddisflies in their casks;*
>
> *warm bubbles released by rotting plants;*
> *distortions cast by the skimmers' dance.*
>
> *Now we throw ourselves against the mountain*
> *and die to spill the symbols we contain!*
>
> *Did we ever love the sea, love gleaning*
> *its deeps? Not now when we're turned to gleaming*
>
> *torpedos. What's it all for if not to leap*
> *upstream to the slopes where firn snows sleep?*

Supply chains synchronize. Ships haul catches
and cargos to shore. Warehousers check

and double-check slips, package, dispatch loads
out every road, while return loads muster

at every road's end. Wheel click, switches
flick in the clockwork. Kona-grown

and Pfizer-synthesized molecules
fuel the citizens' clepsydras, dose diseases,

and their surplus goes drip-drop down pipes –
dispersing, tainting slicks that trickle down

storm drains to bays where gulls rock
on licks of waves.
Time for a magic trick?

Rip up a sheet of text. Slap, spread the scraps
on a tabletop and knead them with both fists.

Next, smooth the confetti with open palms.
Breathe deep. Find the rims and pick it up:

let all witness how the mess has merged
into a brand-new leaf. Unmarked. A flawless,

fog-white page, the same and not the same.
*Tick, tock.*
Who wakes? The moon's disk

dims. Convoys of crows thread up the sky's raw
rim. Gulls shriek applause. The dark winds tick.